Praise for

The Watcher

"Wendy's love for her mother, loyalty to her fatherland, and her wish to keep her mother happy touched me. This book was wonderful."

—Rachel Bolte, Beaufort Elementary School

"[Wendy's] predicament is so interesting . . . does credit to both the author and her readers . . . in this informative adventure."

—*Wall Street Journal*

Also by Joan Hiatt Harlow

Shadows on the Sea (a companion to *The Watcher*)
Star in the Storm
Thunder from the Sea
Blown Away!
Joshua's Song
Midnight Rider
Secret of the Night Ponies
Firestorm

The Watcher

Joan Hiatt Harlow

Margaret K. McElderry Books
New York London Toronto Sydney New Delhi

MARGARET K. McELDERRY BOOKS
An imprint of Simon & Schuster Children's Publishing Division
1230 Avenue of the Americas, New York, New York 10020
This book is a work of fiction. Any references to historical events, real people, or real places are used fictitiously. Other names, characters, places, and events are products of the author's imagination, and any resemblance to actual events or places or persons, living or dead, is entirely coincidental.

For information about special discounts for bulk purchases, please contact Simon & Schuster Special Sales at 1-866-506-1949 or business@simonandschuster.com.
The Simon & Schuster Speakers Bureau can bring authors to your live event. For more information or to book an event, contact the Simon & Schuster Speakers Bureau at 1-866-248-3049 or visit our website at www.simonspeakers.com.
Also available in a Margaret K. McElderry Books hardcover edition
Book design by Sonia Chaghatzbanian and Irene Metaxatos
The text for this book is set in Minion Pro.
Manufactured in the United States of America
First Margaret K. McElderry Books paperback edition November 2015
1015 OFF
10 9 8 7 6 5 4 3 2 1
The Library of Congress has cataloged the hardcover edition as follows:
Harlow, Joan Hiatt.
The watcher / Joan Hiatt Harlow.—First edition.
p. cm.
Companion book to: Shadows on the sea.
Summary: Kidnapped by her own mother, a Nazi spy, teenaged Wendy is transported from Maine to wartime Berlin, where she secretly supports the resistance movement and learns a family secret.
Includes bibliographical references.
ISBN 978-1-4424-2911-6 (hc)
ISBN 978-1-4424-2912-3 (pbk)
ISBN 978-1-4424-2913-0 (eBook)
[1. World War, 1939–1945—Germany—Berlin—Fiction. 2. Nazis—Fiction. 3. Identity—Fiction. 4. Parental kidnapping—Fiction. 5. Mothers and daughters—Fiction. 6. World War, 1939–1945—Underground movements—Germany—Fiction. 7. Germany—History—1933–1945—Fiction.] I. Title.
PZ7.H22666Wat 2014
[Fic]—dc23
2014030259

Für meine sieben Schätzchen
(For my seven little treasures):

Richie
Jack and Sam
Anthony, Abigail, Hope
Owen

Ich hab euch lieb.
(I love you all!)
From Noanie

Contents

The Watcher

sick? You *are* home! This room, this entire house has been waiting for you since you were born. And now, finally, you are home. So why on earth are you crying?"

"I—I'm sorry, Adrie," I stammered. "Everything is happening so . . . fast. I hardly know who I am . . . or where I am. . . ." I tried hard to hold back more tears.

When she spoke again, her voice was icy. "Get this into your head once and for all. You are Wendy Dekker, my daughter. And this"—she stretched out her arms, encompassing the room—"this is your home."

I had no choice after all. It didn't matter if I wanted to go back to the States. It didn't matter if I were scared or homesick or lonesome. I opened my mouth to speak, but she silenced me with her hand, palm up, and came closer.

"Forget the propaganda you've heard back in the States—lies about Germany, Nazis, Hitler, and this war." Then, grabbing a hand mirror from the bedside table, she held it up to my face. "*This* is who you are," Adrie repeated fiercely. "Wendy Dekker."

The girl in the mirror—with teary eyes and a runny nose—was a stranger to me.

Adrie went on. "You are not American and you never were! You are a German girl—*ein Deutsches Mädchen*. Germany is your fatherland and Germany is where your loyalties lie." She opened the curtains wide and pointed to the world outside my window. "And that city out there—Berlin, Germany—is where you—Wendy Dekker—live!"

2
Apology

Was I hearing correctly? Was this the Adrie I had loved so much all my life? I shivered as my brain tried to register her words—her ultimatum to me and my obligations to her.

Adrie is my mother.

I am German.

This house is my home in Berlin, Germany.

Get used to it!

Then Adrie spoke in a gentler voice. "Now, take a bath, get dressed, and then come down to breakfast."

Still stunned and hardly able to speak, I followed her to the bathroom.

"This is your own bathroom," she said. "Everything you need is here. When you are done, come down to the kitchen and meet Frieda, our housekeeper." Adrie left, closing the door behind her. I could hear her footsteps on the stairway.

The bathroom walls were white and sprinkled with blue and white roses. On the shelves were matching towels. Even the soaps were molded into blue flowers.

I turned on the hot water, found a tube of bubble bath in the soap dish, emptied it into the gushing water, and watched it foam. The scent was Lily of the Valley—Mom's favorite perfume—my mom in New York, that is. *I never said good-bye,* I thought as tears welled up again.

I must not cry. I must not!

I pulled off my socks and thought about the German sailor who had given them to me to keep my feet warm on the submarine. He was as handsome and young and just as sweet as any American boys I knew. I didn't hate him because he was German. He didn't hate me because I was American. Why did there have to be a war?

Then I remembered Adrie's words: *You are not American and you never were.*

I climbed into the tub and sank under the fragrant bubbles. *Maybe everything will be all right,* I told myself. *Maybe I'll be fine here in my new life once I get used to it.*

I had no other choice, anyway.

After washing and rinsing my hair, I climbed out of the tub and wrapped myself in a thick white bathrobe that hung on the door. I tiptoed across the hall to my bedroom and came to an abrupt stop in the open doorway. A woman was sitting on my bed, rummaging through my backpack!

"What are you doing?" I demanded.

Startled, she jumped from the bed, spilling some of the contents of my backpack onto the floor. She muttered something in German and hastily gathered up my belongings.

I dashed to the bed and grabbed my things out of the woman's hands. "Why are you poking through my stuff?"

At that moment, Adrie entered the room. "What's going on?"

"This woman was looking through my backpack."

"Wendy, this is Frieda," Adrie said.

"She was going through my things."

Frieda and Adrie began speaking to each other in German.

"Speak in English," I insisted angrily. "It's as if I'm not even here when you chatter to each other in German."

Adrie put her hand up, telling me to be quiet. "Frieda does not speak English, and you upset her with your attitude. Now apologize, please."

"She should apologize to me. She's the one who—"

Adrie interrupted and glared at me. "Frieda has been in this household for years. I would trust her with my life. Now, apologize to Frieda."

I plopped into a nearby chair. "I've only just arrived in this household. No one told me she's allowed to—"

"Apologize!" Adrie demanded.

I looked up at the housekeeper. "I'm sorry, Frieda—"

"*Entschuldigung*," Adrie interrupted. "It means you're sorry. Repeat after me: Ent-shul-digung."

I struggled to say the German word then waited for Frieda's reaction.

She simply nodded, folded the clothes that had fallen,

set them on top of the dresser, and left the room.

"You insulted her," Adrie snapped. Before she left the bedroom, she added, "Bring those things that Frieda left on the dresser. She will iron them up nicely, and they will do for today."

I picked up the one skirt I had brought. It was plain dark blue and so crumpled from being stuffed into my backpack that I was sure no one would be able to iron it smooth again. The white blouse with blue buttons that went with it was just as wrinkled.

After my outburst at Frieda, I hated to face her. However, I followed Adrie downstairs and into the kitchen. Frieda was standing by the stove. I tried to smile as I handed her my wrinkled clothes.

She gave me a long look, took the clothing, and disappeared into another part of the house, off the kitchen.

It's my first day in Berlin, and I've already made an enemy, I thought miserably.

3
Shopping Spree

Adrie brought me into the dining room and handed me a framed photograph of a handsome German officer. "This was your father, Karl Dekker," she said. "He was a loyal officer in the Great War. Sadly, he was badly injured and never got over his wounds. He died when you were about six."

I concentrated on my father's face, trying to see similarities to myself—maybe the shape of his nose or the arch of his brows—but there were none. I was looking at a total stranger. His expression reminded me of the pictures of German officers I had seen—determined, resolute.

I handed the picture back to Adrie, who placed it carefully on the walnut armoire. "Did he know . . . about me?"

"Of course. He was always interested in how you were growing and what you were doing."

"Was he a nice man, Adrie?"

"Oh, yes. He was a fine German officer."

I already knew that. In fact, that was all I knew. What I wanted to hear was what he was really like. Was he kind? Was he gentle? Was he funny? Would I have loved him? Would he have loved me?

We went out to the terrace, where Frieda had set up a breakfast of pancakes and sausages for me. Adrie had already eaten, but she sat opposite me drinking a cup of coffee. The food was delicious and I was so hungry, I asked for seconds.

I said, *"Sehr gut, Frieda,"* which Adrie told me to say and means "very good." I hoped Frieda knew I meant it.

Shortly after breakfast, Frieda brought the skirt and blouse to me—all beautifully pressed and ready to wear. *"Danke,"* I said with a big smile. I had come to realize how *sehr gut* it was to have Frieda cooking and ironing for us.

Adrie went inside to dress, and I was alone on the terrace. The table was set under a maroon-and-white-striped awning that extended the length of the terrace. Although the July morning was hot, under that awning it was cool and comfortable.

Across the street was a park surrounded by a black wrought-iron fence that stretched all the way up to the next street. The tall lush green trees of the park stirred in the light summer breeze, and the sun sent shadows through the leaves.

Suddenly, for an instant, as the wind parted the branches and foliage behind the park fence, I saw a face! I stood up, straining to see better, but just as quickly, the branches and leaves gathered together and the face was gone.

It must have been an illusion, I told myself. The sun and the shadows, along with moving leaves had given me the impression of a face. That was all it was—an illusion. I shivered and brushed the eerie feeling aside.

Adrie and I took the bus to the Wertheim department store in the Leipziger Platz. The store filled up at least two or three blocks, and looked about six stories high—almost like a city by itself.

"This is the largest department store in Europe," Adrie told me when we stepped off the bus.

Canvas canopies, painted with green leaves and branches, hung above the sidewalks along the wide street, concealing the sky. "From the air, this looks like a forest," Adrie explained. "If enemy planes come, they'll never know this is downtown Berlin."

"Has Berlin been bombed?" I asked.

"Yes, we were bombed, but it wasn't much of anything. However, it angered our Führer, and he ordered forty days of bombing Britain. The British called it 'the Blitz.'"

"Oh, I saw pictures of the Blitz in the news. The Germans bombed homes and hospitals—"

"Served them right," Adrie interrupted. "The British won't be trying that again."

"I hope not." After all, I lived in Berlin now.

Once inside the store, it was easy to put the war, bombs, and fear aside. I loved to shop, and needed many things.

We started with underwear, and Adrie bought lovely undies, nighties, and pajamas for me. Then we moved on to the next department and picked out shoes, then sweaters and a jacket.

I hated the black shorts and white sleeveless shirts with black swastikas on them, and those ugly brown skirts that were the proper uniforms for girls. "I don't want to join those groups," I said. But then I added quickly, "Considering that I cannot speak German, the girls will know I'm American, and they'll hate me."

"You'll learn our language quickly because you are living here now. It's the way babies learn to speak. They hear a language over and over, and before long they've mastered it."

"Isn't there something else I can do here instead of joining a girls' youth group?"

"We'll talk about it later."

I was disappointed when she purchased the uniforms anyway.

In the dress shop, Adrie bought me skirts and shirts and an adorable red-and-green-striped peasant dress with a white bodice and puffed sleeves, with an attached lace-trimmed apron.

"You are a true German in this Bavarian *dirndl*, with your blond hair and blue eyes," Adrie said with an approving nod. "Now we'll have lunch at the little café on the first floor."

We sat in a booth and ordered chicken salad—*Huehner Salat*—and tea.

"The government took ownership of this store because it was originally owned by Jews," Adrie explained as we waited for our order. "Now all the employees and buyers are Aryans."

"Why did they take away this store from Jewish owners?"

"Jews are outlawed in Germany now. In fact, it is a crime for Germans to marry Jews. You should keep that in mind."

"I have no intentions of marrying anyone. I'm not even fifteen yet."

"In any case, you are a German—an Aryan—and you need to keep that blood pure."

I had no idea who the Aryans were, but I didn't need to ask because Adrie was about to tell me.

"Aryans are a purebred race that lived years ago. Scandinavians and Germans, and some English, too, are descendants of that perfect race. Usually they are handsome, blond, blue-eyed, and fair skinned, like you." She leaned over the table and spoke with a fervor I didn't understand.

"Above all things remember this: You have pure German blood for many generations on both sides of your family." Adrie sat back and folded her hands. "Don't ever forget. This is your heritage because you are one hundred percent German."

"I won't forget, Adrie," I promised. *How could I forget when she keeps telling me all the time?*

◉◉

We had so many packages, we took a taxi home. Frieda met us at the door and helped me carry my packages up to my room.

Frieda had been cooking all the time we were gone, and something smelled delicious. We sat down at the oak table in the kitchen while Frieda ladled out beef stew into white bowls and set them on the table. Then she cut fresh bread that she had made herself, and served it on a platter next to a crock of butter.

"Butter?" I asked, looking at Adrie. Back in the States, it was practically impossible to buy butter since the war.

Adrie nodded. "The real thing—not that awful white margarine substitute. I am able, fortunately, to buy many luxuries. I'm rewarded well for the work that I do." She took a slice of bread, spread it thick with butter, and placed it on my dish. "Here you go. Enjoy it."

I didn't know exactly what Adrie did for work—but this wasn't the time to ask and I was too hungry to care. The stew was thick with meat, carrots, potatoes, and cabbage. I hadn't had a real substantial meal with meat in a long time—not even back in the States—but we didn't lack anything here, and I devoured two bowlfuls.

After a dessert of baked cinnamon apples topped with sweet nutty syrup and whipped cream, Adrie said, "Tomorrow you will come with me to my office downtown. There you will meet Admiral Canaris, who is—as you say in America—my boss."

Although I was curious about Adrie's work, I was sure I'd be bored. "Are you positive you want me to go with you?"

"Of course. I'm positive. Admiral Canaris often asks about you. I was told he has a surprise for us."

"A surprise? For us?"

"Yes. But now it's time for you to go to bed." She stood up, dismissing me.

I would have liked to stay up longer, but I could tell Adrie was finished with me. It was as if she were checking me off her list of daily duties.

"Thank you for all the beautiful clothes you bought me, Adrie," I said before leaving.

"You're welcome," she answered. "Sleep well."

I went to my room, put on my new pajamas, turned out the light, and looked out the window. My room faced the park, which was dark now. For a moment I recalled the face I had seen amid the foliage. *It was simply a mirage,* I told myself as I climbed into bed.

Still, it really had looked like a face.

4
Speeding on the Autobahn

The next morning after breakfast, Adrie reminded me of our visit to meet with Admiral Canaris. I hoped it wouldn't take long.

"How come Admiral Canaris isn't on a ship? An admiral is a naval officer, isn't it?"

"He was in the navy in the last war. Now he is the head the *Abwehr* military intelligence unit."

"Intelligence? Does that mean he's a genius or something?"

Adrie laughed. "Well, he is a brilliant man, actually," she explained, still chuckling. "He has a position of great importance. *Abwehr* is the department that hunts out those who are working against our Führer."

Things were beginning to fall into place. Adrie was a spy and she worked for the German government as a spy in the United States. They had found out and wanted to catch her. And that was the reason we had to run away.

"Oh, so *Abwehr* is a spy organization?" I asked.

"Go get dressed and don't ask so many questions."

I wore a new blue skirt, shirt, and jacket along with matching shoes, and Adrie wore a deep blue suit, so we sort of matched. She called a taxi, and we drove through downtown Berlin to the *Abwehr* office. Of course, there was no sign on the door advertising the fact that this was a Nazi spy organization. It didn't seem different than any other office that I'd seen. However, there were signs on some doors that indicated no one was allowed through unless they had priority clearance. Adrie translated for me.

I think I was expecting the need for a top-secret code to open the door, or a bookcase that swung open to a hidden room. But then, when I looked at Adrie, she wasn't like a spy I might have seen in a movie. I didn't think she ever had one of those spy raincoats with lots of pockets or a wristwatch that was really a radio. She looked more like a professional journalist or maybe the president of some big company.

Admiral Canaris was a small man, quiet-spoken, and very sweet. He didn't seem to me one bit like a top spy person—or whatever his title was. He smiled and shook my hand firmly and spoke softly to Adrie. She told him I didn't speak German, and he nodded agreeably. They spoke back and forth, and I could tell some of the conversation was about me because they would look at me. I heard the word *Unterseeboot* and knew Adrie was telling him about our trip across the ocean in the submarine.

After some conversation between them, I noticed a look of surprise, followed by disappointment on Adrie's face. *What had he told her that caused her distress?* I wondered.

Admiral Canaris then took a key from his desk and motioned for us to follow him outside to the parking lot at the back of the building. He took us to a shiny two-door silver-gray car. He unlocked the doors and motioned for Adrie to get into the driver's seat. Admiral Canaris stood by, explaining various switches and gears and turning on the windshield wipers, the lights, and the horn. Adrie started the engine, and after she said *danke* a dozen or more times, I realized then that he had given her the car.

The admiral opened the passenger-side door and signaled for me to get in. Then, standing back, he gave us a little salute, pointed to the driveway, and went back into the building.

"This was the surprise. We have an auto!" Adrie whispered. "And what a beauty!"

"It looks brand-new," I said, admiring the leather seats and shiny knobs and equipment. "What kind of car is it?"

"It's a 1939 Opel Kapitän. There haven't been new cars in Germany since 1940. Now we don't need to call a taxi for every little thing." Adrie concentrated as she drove out to the road and pulled in to a line of traffic.

"How come he gave it to you?"

She shrugged and raised her eyebrows. "I guess I can thank you for this. Since you are living with me now, he thinks it will be better that I don't travel outside of Germany for a while."

"Because of me?"

"Well, not just because of you," she explained. "It's more likely because my face has been plastered all over newspapers in America and England since we were nearly captured back in Maine. It would be dangerous for me to work outside of Germany now. In any case, he gave me the car for everyday use, as well as for future *Abwehr* assignments I might have in this country."

As we turned onto the Autobahn, the busy highway Hitler had built, Adrie gave a little whistle. "This is a powerful car. It's one of the last government-owned automobiles. There aren't many left, so I'm fortunate to get this beauty. It will make up somewhat for the projects I was hoping to get."

Projects she hoped to get. So it was because of me that she wouldn't get them.

Adrie shifted gears and stepped hard on the accelerator. "Hang on to your hat!"

I held my breath as we zoomed off, passing all the other speeding cars on the Autobahn.

5
Deadly Dogs

We had been driving for an hour or so, and I wondered where we were going. After several minutes Adrie glanced at her watch and said, "I do have to see someone up the road here—about work."

"Oh, do you have to?" I complained, and then fearing she would be angry, I added, "I was hoping we could do something—just the two of us—like yesterday."

"It's essential that I deal with some important things while we are here." She turned a corner and came to a stop outside a large facility. "I have an idea. You might be interested in seeing how SS police dogs are trained for service. It will give you something to do while you're waiting for me."

Adrie took me into a building and spoke to an officer behind the desk. Then she said to me, "You are invited to watch while those uniformed men work with the dogs." As she turned to go she added, "Oh, I told them you don't speak German. They'll have someone speak to you in English."

The man behind the desk motioned for me to come with him. We walked out onto a pathway that wound among the buildings in the complex and where armed men in SS uniforms patrolled with their dogs.

In the field beyond the compound, a dog crouched by its trainer, waiting for a signal. Then, upon command, the animal, its teeth bared, darted toward a humanlike dummy that stood on the other side of the field. In an instant the dog leaped, knocked the dummy to the ground, and began tearing it to shreds. I cringed at the sound of gnashing teeth and snarls.

Why are these dogs being taught to kill? Did Adrie really think I would find this fun to watch? I winced as, on command, the dogs, fur bristled, bodies tensed, sprang on men who wore protective clothing and played the parts of the prisoner or enemy.

The officer who was with me stopped and spoke to me in English. "Perhaps you'd like to see the puppies we are training."

I followed him to a long narrow building where various-size dogs peered out from kennels. The officer opened a cage where the smallest puppies squealed, scurried out to me, and licked my hands as I stooped to pet them.

"They're adorable," I murmured. "I hate to think they'll be vicious police dogs soon."

One shy black-brown-and-white puppy stood off, eyeing us. "What are you doing there all by yourself? Just watching?" I called. "Come see me, little guy."

The guard snickered. "He won't come. He's stupid—not good for anything."

"Come on, little pup," I crooned. "You want to play, don't you?" This time, I could see the puppy's eyes brighten—and he pounced over to me.

"Ha!" said the officer. "He likes you."

When I knelt to pet him, the little dog rubbed against me as if looking for affection, his tail wagging madly. I put my arms around him, and he jumped up immediately and lapped my face. "I love this one!"

"Oh, that dog is worthless," the officer scoffed. "Look at him. He doesn't lift his ears upright like a pure-blooded noble German shepherd."

Sure enough. Instead of straight perked-up ears, one of this dog's ears folded over comically.

"Why do you say he's worthless? Surely, it has nothing to do with his ears."

"He's a clown. He doesn't obey, and he's six months old. I expect he'll be put down sometime soon."

"What do you mean 'put down'?"

"He'll probably be shot," the man replied. "We can't afford to train and feed a dog that is of no use. If a dog can't be trained, he's shot. That's it."

I took ahold of the dog's collar and pulled him closer to me. The dog's cold nose tickled my neck as he climbed back into my arms. "No, he can't be shot," I objected loudly. "He's a wonderful dog. Someone would want him."

"Do you want him?" the officer asked. "You can have him, but you need to remember we are at war and a pet takes many of your rations. You may be sorry."

"I'll speak to my mother when she returns," I said, holding the puppy close.

I won't let them shoot this dog! I have to convince Adrie to let me keep him.

6
Promises

When Adrie walked through the door, the dog was sleeping in my lap. "Are you ready to leave?"

"I don't know."

Adrie frowned. "What do you mean, you don't know?"

"Oh, Adrie, I can't leave this dog here. They're going to shoot him."

"Why are they going to shoot him?"

"Because he's not vicious enough to be a police dog, that's why." I waited for a response, but Adrie looked befuddled, so I pressed on. "He's a beautiful, lovable puppy, and they're going to kill him. Can we take him with us?"

"No, we can't. We absolutely cannot!"

"Please . . ."

"It is selfish to take on a dog during wartime. The dog has to be fed, and that takes food away from our soldiers." She gestured for me to go to the door.

"Adrie, I'd willingly go without food myself to feed him. Just look at him." I pointed to him cuddled so sweetly in my lap. "He doesn't want to be vicious or to kill. He only wants to be loved."

"It's impossible. Where would we keep him? Who would take care of him?"

"I would, of course! Oh, please, please, Adrie."

"No. Absolutely not." She headed for the door, expecting me to follow.

I didn't move. "I found a puppy who needs a friend, just like I do. I don't know anyone here in Germany. I have no friends. I can't speak German. I would be so happy if I could have this dog." The pup looked up at Adrie and yawned sleepily. "The officer said I could have him. So please, please let me take him home. We can't leave him here to be shot."

Adrie sighed and rolled her eyes. "I never should have let you wait for me here with these puppies. I thought you'd find it interesting, but I never expected . . ." She took ahold of my arm and pulled me up. "Come on. We're leaving—without that dog!"

The puppy, who had slipped off my lap onto the floor, sat and watched us with the saddest expression. "No, I'm not going." I dropped to my knees and threw both arms around the dog. "I won't leave him to be shot."

"So you're telling me that you are going to stay here, by yourself, if I don't let you have that dog. Is that what you're saying?" Adrie's anger was about to erupt.

"Adrie," I pleaded. "I've come here to Germany to be

with you. I gave up my family and friends to be with you. I crossed the ocean in a U-boat that was torpedoed, because I wanted to be with you. I'm asking only that you will let me have this dog. I will take care of him, I promise! I'll clean up after him, walk him, train him, and do everything. You won't even know he's around. Oh, don't you see? I . . . I need him. And he needs me, too."

Surprisingly, the SS Officer who had taken me on the tour of the facility spoke up. "This dog would make a good pet," he said to Adrie. "He's not vicious and it looks like they've taken to each other."

Adrie replied angrily in German and shook her finger in his face.

The officer put his hand up for her to stop and barked at her in English, "For the love of God, shut up and let her have the dog!"

Adrie looked stunned. Then as if conceding defeat, she shrugged. "Oh, all right. I guess we can take him."

"Thank you, thank you!" I jumped to my feet and reached out to Adrie, who allowed herself to be hugged. "I promise I'll take him for walks and feed him and brush him . . . and . . ."

"Yes, you will," Adrie agreed, shoving me away. "And without one single complaint."

"I promise! I promise!"

7
Mean and Catty

I sat in the backseat of the car with the puppy on my lap. He was sweet, and every so often he looked up happily and lapped my hands or my face. I thought of my daddy back home, and how he always wanted a German shepherd.

Adrie was silent, and I was worried about her attitude toward me—and my puppy—once we got home. I hoped she was so happy with the car, she would forget about being angry with me.

Adrie finally looked at me through the rearview mirror. "We have an invitation to tea at three o'clock, and I have made a reservation. Ironically, it is a mother-and-daughter affair, and the first time ever you and I could go to something like this as mother and daughter. But now you have this dog. So what will we do with him while we attend the tea?"

I didn't care about a tea party at all, but I could tell it was important to Adrie. "Can't we just leave him in the car with the windows open a bit?"

"I don't want him clawing the upholstery, or messing in the car!"

"I'll come out and take him for walks," I said. "We won't be gone long, will we?"

"I don't know how long we'll be gone, and I don't want to hurry. There are girls there your age who are daughters of my friends. You said you had no friends, so this is your chance—and the girls are waiting to meet you."

We pulled in to the driveway of a large restaurant and drove to the back, where several other cars were parked. Adrie pulled off the pavement and stopped near a grove of trees. Then we opened the windows just enough for my puppy to get a sniff of air.

Adrie locked the car, and we headed into the restaurant. I looked back and could see my pup watching me from the window. His eyes were sad, and I could hear him whining.

Inside, a waitress dressed in a *dirndl* dress and apron led us into a private banquet room where a group of women and girls were mingling and talking. There were only women there, and most of the daughters were younger than I was—under ten, I was sure. There were only a few girls my age.

I felt ill at ease and awkward. I knew Adrie would have to explain that I spoke only English since I was brought up in the United States. I was sure that fact would immediately make enemies for me.

Adrie put her arm around me and introduced me to various women she knew. I just curtsied and smiled as Adrie had advised earlier. I could tell many women were surprised to learn that Adrie had a daughter at all. Then she had to explain that I was her daughter from America and that I did not speak German.

Adrie wasn't intimidated by questions. I knew she was telling them about our trip across the Atlantic in a submarine when she used the word *Unterseeboot.*

When they heard this and asked many questions, Adrie translated for me.

How exciting that I had had a trip in the *Unterseeboot.* Had I been afraid? Did I get seasick?

When would I join the girls' youth group?

One of the women, Frau Himmelman, asked another question, and when Adrie answered *"vierzehn,"* I recognized, from the few German courses I'd taken in school, the word *fourteen.*

She must have asked my age, because Adrie answered, "Fourteen."

I tapped Adrie's arm. "You forgot. I'll be fifteen next week."

"That's right." Adrie laughed and corrected herself. *"Fünfzehn heute. Geburtstag."*

This brought a chorus of congratulations and a few kisses on my cheek.

"Alles Gute zum Geburtstag."

Immediately the woman beckoned two teenage girls who were watching from across the room. *"Kommt hier her."*

The two girls looked at each other, raised their eyebrows, and sauntered over to the group.

Adrie whispered, "She wants to introduce you since they're your age."

Once again, the German words flew around. The girls quickly smirked, and I nodded, not knowing what was being said other than an introduction.

Adrie then explained in English. "This is Rikka, Frau Himmelman's daughter. She belongs to the young German girls' group." Rikka was tall and slim as a rake handle, and her tight curly brown hair looked as if she just had gotten a permanent wave. She smiled at me and stepped back. Both girls wore the *dirndl* dresses so popular in Germany. I wished that I had worn mine.

"This is Gertrude Ernst," Adrie said, gesturing to the other girl whose thick braids wound around her head and framed her perfectly round face. "And this is Frau Ernst, her mother. She is a pediatric doctor."

Frau Ernst smiled and nodded, then reached out to bring her daughter closer to our group.

I almost laughed when I saw the resemblance between Gertrude and her mother. Both wore braids circling their heads, and their round faces both reminded me of gingerbread men—same smile, same raisin eyes.

Almost immediately Gertrude burst into a string of loud, fast sentences. Frau Ernst poked her daughter, but the girl kept talking.

When Gertrude stopped for a breath, Adrie spoke rapidly in German, and I noticed a tone of annoyance in her voice. The grown-ups looked at one another with raised eyebrows as the two girls turned abruptly and went back to their former place at the end of the room.

Frau Ernst, looking embarrassed, spoke softly to Adrie. I recognized a familiar German word: *Entschuldigung*. I remembered that word only too well. It meant, apologize. I was sure Gertrude had said something rude to me, and now her mother was apologizing to Adrie.

These girls are mean and catty—just like that group of girls in Maine. I hoped never to have to see them again.

Still, I wondered what Gertrude had said.

8
A Watcher

I was relieved when Adrie finally suggested we go home. I prayed there would be no more tea parties for me to attend, especially any with Rikka and Gertrude.

My puppy was asleep when we got back to the car. "Look, he didn't mess in the car; he didn't chew the upholstery. Isn't he a good puppy, Adrie?"

"Take him for a quick walk right now so there won't be any accidents on the way home," Adrie ordered.

I clamped on the leash the SS officer had given me, and the puppy jumped onto the grass. He sniffed around, as dogs do, and before long, he was ready to get into the car again.

"Come on, little guy," I said as I settled him into the backseat. "We're taking you to our beautiful new home. You and I both have a new home. Aren't we lucky?" I said this for Adrie's sake, but she didn't seem to notice. "What is our address?" I asked Adrie. "I don't even know."

"*Sieben Lindenstrasse*," Adrie answered. "Seven Linden Street. *Sieben Lindenstrasse*."

"*Sieben . . . Linden . . . strasse*," I muttered. "*Sieben Lindenstrasse*."

Before long, we turned onto our street and pulled in to the driveway. I gathered my puppy into my arms and got out. Then, stopping on the walkway, I looked at the stone house with its formal elegance. It was certainly beautiful, and I felt a tinge of emotion for the father I never met. He would be happy to know I was actually here in my own home at last.

Adrie hustled up the steps, her key in hand, but before she could slip it into the lock, Frieda opened the door and the puppy squirmed from my arms and tumbled into the foyer.

At first Frieda looked surprised and startled. Would she mind my having the dog? Would she complain to Adrie? As the puppy jumped and wiggled at her feet, Frieda bent down as if to quiet him. The pup had other ideas. He leaped up and licked Frieda's face, his tail wagging like a flag in a gale. Frieda looked stunned as she wiped her face with her apron.

"Quite an introduction," Adrie muttered, shaking her head. "We should have prepared Frieda for this . . . animal."

I picked the puppy up and brought him into the kitchen. Adrie and Frieda followed, and I could tell by the tone of her voice that Adrie was apologizing for the dog. After a short conversation back and forth in German,

Adrie said to me, "The dog will stay here in the kitchen and sleep under the table. Frieda has an old blanket for him. You will need to take him out at night before we all go to bed and first thing in the morning, too. That's your job, Wendy, not Frieda's."

"I know. I will, I promise."

Frieda scooped out meat and vegetables from a pot on the stove and put it in a dish. To my surprise, she set it on the floor. The pup sniffed the dish and then chomped the food down happily. When he was finished and looked up, even Adrie laughed at the gravy all over his nose.

Frieda had prepared a luscious supper. The beef roast was so tender, it fell apart with a fork. It was surrounded with potatoes, onions, carrots, and cabbage. Frieda watched with a satisfied smile as I helped myself to seconds.

"*Rinderbraten mit Gemüse,*" Frieda said slowly and clearly.

"*Rinderbraten mit Gemüse,*" I repeated with my mouth full. "*Gut.*"

"That's roast beef with vegetables," Adrie translated. "We have this meat only because of my position with the *Abwehr*," she explained. "Rationing now allows only one-tenth of a pound of meat per person per day." She gave me a meaningful look. "Having a dog is almost sinful when people are hungry."

"Then I'll share my food with him," I told her.

I could tell Frieda was trying to please me as she hovered around, placing warm, buttered rolls on my plate and filling my glass with milk whenever it was even partly empty. But I wondered how she really felt about my bringing a dog into the house. I knew Frieda had a lot of influence with Adrie. Meanwhile, the puppy curled up under the table at my feet and fell asleep.

"I hope you can train this dog to be obedient," Adrie said to me later. "You can't expect Frieda to take charge of him."

"It's my dog. I don't expect anyone to take care of him. I'm sure he'll be easy to train," I assured her.

"Well, the SS officers didn't think he was easy to train. Do you think you're better than they are?"

"They weren't showing love to him. He'll obey when he knows he's loved, because he'll want to please me. He's a good dog, Adrie, you'll see." I had an idea. "I notice what a large library you have. Would there be a book there on training dogs?"

"Karl had a dog for a while—a little squeaky thing—a dachshund, I think. There might be a book on dog training in our library. Most likely it would be in German. Still, you could look and see."

Earlier I had peeked into the library room, but I had not had time to get a good look at the shelves of books that lined the walls. I hoped there were some books in English.

After dinner I went to the library, which was accessible from the front hall or from the French doors that led out to the terrace. Even with the two large French doors open facing the western sun, the library was a dark room with its mahogany furniture and paneling. I turned on several lights and glanced at the bookshelves that stretched up to the high ceiling. *How would anyone get books from those shelves?* I wondered. I could see a track around the shelves, indicating there had once been a library ladder, but now I didn't see one.

At that moment Adrie came into the library to see what I was doing.

"Is there a library ladder to get around the upper shelves?" I asked.

"There is one in the closet. However, it is broken and I haven't had a chance to get it fixed. I put it in the closet so no one would try to use it and get hurt. Please use only the shelves that you can reach."

"Okay," I said.

"Remember, you must use only the lower shelves," she repeated. "There are no books up high that you would be interested in anyway. They're all in German or other languages." Adrie turned to leave then stopped. "Do you understand?"

"Yes, I understand," I said.

Adrie's collections of books were in a dozen or more languages, but I was able to find two books on learning German from English. *I'd like to learn German secretly,* I thought. *Then I can surprise Adrie.* And I'd also know what was being said about me—like what that girl Gertrude who was at the tea party had said. I set the books on the desk to take upstairs later.

I was about to look for books about training dogs

when a crow or a jay screamed out from across the street. Startled, I turned sharply to the open doors, which faced the park. The shrubs near the park fence shook as the bird flew off. I warily stared at the darkening trees on the other side of the iron fence. The sun was about to set, and the shadows were deepening. Suddenly a shadowy silhouette moved among the bushes and trees.

Was it just another illusion from the setting sun and the wind stirring the leaves?

I waited, wondering when . . . there it was again! This time I could make out the clear outline of a person, a man standing on the other side of the fence, looking directly at me! Whoever it was swiftly backed away into the foliage and disappeared from view.

I felt goose bumps prickle my arms, and I rushed to shut the French doors, lock them, and pull the heavy drapes over the glass panes.

Was it just a passerby in the park? Someone who simply happened to glance at the lighted room? No, this was different—deliberate. Someone was out there watching this house—watching me.

9
Nighttime Concerns

For a moment I froze and waited, watching between a slit in the drapes. Whoever was out there had retreated into the shrubbery and disappeared. This was not an illusion. I clearly saw the figure of a man, and I was sure I had seen someone in the park before, and thought it was my imagination.

I ran from the library and into Adrie's den where she did her work and kept files. She was listening to the news on the radio. The announcer spoke excitedly in German.

"Adrie! Someone is watching our house. I've seen him twice now."

Adrie turned the volume down. "Who's watching us?"

"I don't know, but it looked like a man."

Adrie listened attentively as I explained how I had seen someone earlier and thought it was just my imagination. Nevertheless, tonight it was clearly the silhouette of a man.

Adrie frowned and appeared thoughtful. "How old a man was he? Could you tell?"

"I didn't see him clearly. Just his form, and then he was gone."

Adrie was silent for a moment, and then she said, "Well, we are supposed to keep the drapes drawn at night in case of air raids. If we follow that law, it will keep Peeping Toms from looking into our house."

"Air raids? I thought Berlin wouldn't get bombed."

"Oh, Wendy, we are at war. We are required to block out the lights. We had the same law back in Maine. Just keep the drapes drawn. Personally, I think you're overtired and that's why you're seeing things." She glanced at her wristwatch. "You should go to bed soon."

"All right." I was about to leave, when she called me back.

"Before you go to bed, be sure to let the dog out for a little while. By the way, he'd better be quiet, because if he whines or cries all night, he'll have to go."

She had turned the radio up again. I nodded and left the room. If Adrie wasn't concerned about the watcher in the park, I guess I shouldn't be concerned either. However, I was worried about the puppy. I hadn't thought about him howling at night, and now Adrie had threatened to get rid of him if he did.

Before going upstairs, I took the puppy out to the backyard, where he sniffed around. After he was finished, I brought him to the blanket Frieda had folded under the table. Frieda watched as I pushed him gently down onto the blanket. "Go to sleep now. Please don't make a sound," I whispered, kissing his head. "I hope you won't be lonely. Tomorrow I will give you a name."

The puppy got up immediately and followed me to the dining-room door.

"No, no. You must stay," I told him. I carried him back to the blanket, but again he followed me to the door and looked at me with mournful eyes.

I could see Frieda watching without any expression. What was she thinking? Did she want the puppy gone? After all, he was in her kitchen, and she might consider him a pest. Once more I pulled him back under the table and set him on the blanket. "Now listen. You have to stay here." I started to leave and he got up. "No, lie down," I insisted.

Adrie called from the hall. "Your dog may understand only German."

"Aha!" Frieda exclaimed. *"Platz!"*

This time the puppy folded his legs and lay down, but he watched me dejectedly as I left the room and closed the door.

Late in the night I was roused by a howling—a deep sad cry. I sat up in bed, wondering for a moment where I was. The whining turned into a sharp bark, and I realized it was the puppy downstairs in the kitchen. If the dog woke up Adrie, she would be furious.

Again the pup howled, louder this time. I climbed out of bed and made my way in the dark to the hall and stairwell. I felt my way along with my hands, not wanting to turn on the lights.

Yelp! Arooo! Yelp! Arooo! The puppy cried then moaned so sadly.

Nothing shone through the draped windows, and not a light was on anywhere. I crept slowly through the pitch black, and down the winding stairway to the first floor, and then headed for the kitchen.

Now the sounds had stopped. I waited. Silence. *Should I go back to bed? What if he began to bark again?*

As I entered the dining room, I noticed a light gleaming from under the door. Quietly, I treaded toward the kitchen and opened the swinging door. No one was there—and the dog was gone.

Another light gleamed from the wing where Frieda slept. Could the puppy have gone into Frieda's room? I tiptoed into the tiled hallway. A door was partly open, and a soft light came from within.

I knocked gently on the door. "Frieda?"

To my surprise, Frieda opened the door and laughed softly. Then with her finger to her lips, she pointed to her bed.

Curled up smack in the center of a soft quilt, his head between his paws and his eyes closed, the puppy snored softly.

I put out my hands to Frieda. "Shall I take him?" I asked, hoping she understood.

She obviously did understand. She shook her head and once again put her hand to her lips. "*Nein,*" she said. And with a smile, she shoved me gently out the door. "*Gute Nacht.*"

My suspicions of Frieda disappeared in an instant. "Good night and *danke*. Thank you," was all that I could say.

10
At the Park

Frieda served breakfast on the beautiful patio the next morning. The summer air was drenched with the scent of flowers. It was a sunny beautiful day, and once again the war seemed faraway.

Frieda brought the newspaper and coffee on a tray. My puppy came running and leaping when he saw me. He sat at my feet, his tail wagging, and his eyes were on my face, watching my every move.

"I should take the dog out," I said, remembering my promise.

"Frieda said she let him out in the fenced-in yard." Adrie unfolded the morning paper. "Wendy, this isn't Frieda's job. It's yours."

"I know, but she beat me to it."

Frieda came out again with a tray of sausage, cheese, toast, and more coffee, and I looked at her anxiously. Had she told Adrie that the dog had slept in her room, in her bed? I hoped not. However, Frieda smiled and winked at me, indicating everything was fine.

Tonight I will have to do something if he starts barking, I decided. *Maybe I'll sneak him up to my room. I can't expect Frieda to take care of him again.*

"I have to decide on a name for my dog," I said to Adrie. "But I don't know what to call him."

"Max is a good name for a dog," Adrie suggested. "It's masculine and strong. I like it."

"Hmm." I wanted something less common than Max. I stood up and gazed out over the patio. "Maybe I'll take him for a walk in the park."

"That's a good idea. And you'll have the dog with you for protection." Adrie laughed. "I don't think Max would be much protection, though, since he failed his police course."

"He'll be a wonderful watchdog. You'll see."

The dog at my side suddenly froze and the hair on his shoulders and back stood up.

He lowered his head as if to get a better look at something. He growled—a soft, low growl—not much louder than a cat's purr.

I followed his gaze and noticed a young man walking his dog on the sidewalk across the street. "You are a good watchdog," I told him. As I patted his ears, the puppy relaxed, looked up, and wagged his tail. "That's what I'll name you," I exclaimed. "Watcher!"

"Watcher is a perfect name," Adrie agreed. "Though

another name beginning with *W*—how difficult you make it for our German friends."

After breakfast Adrie had work to do in her den, so she didn't seem to mind that I was taking a walk. Of course, I didn't let on that I was determined to look for footprints or any clue to where that Peeping Tom had stood and what he might have been looking at—other than me.

I fastened a leash to Watcher's collar. The puppy jumped, wagged his tail, and eagerly tugged me along. "Heel!" I commanded with a tug on the leash. Watcher ignored me, sniffed at nearby plants, and strained to run after squirrels.

I knelt down, held Watcher by his collar, and looked directly into his eyes. "Listen to me, Watcher," I said in a stern voice. "I know we speak different languages, but I'm sure you can see I'm serious. Now, walk with me quietly and quit pulling me in other directions."

I got up and continued down the sidewalk. This time, to my surprise, Watcher trotted along next to me and only occasionally focused on a blowing leaf or shadow.

We strolled along behind our house where the iron fence of the park separated the trees and gardens from the sidewalk. Once we turned the corner, I could see the entrance to the park. The tall black iron gate was open, so we went inside. A few mothers and nursemaids pushed carriages through the pleasant surroundings. Water gushed from the mouth of a fish statue that stood in a fountain by the entrance.

The July morning was hot, so I sat on a bench by a pool

to cool off after our walk. A little boy placed a paper boat into the pool, but it quickly sank in the rushing water. He began to cry, and his nurse picked him up and rocked him. But his screaming was disturbing, and Watcher whined and pulled at the leash in an effort to get to the child.

I stood up to explore the area that would be directly behind the terrace of our house, and once I gave Watcher a little tug, he trotted alongside obediently.

The walking paths were set out from the fountain like spokes on a wheel. The trail to the right seemed to wind its way around the perimeter, so I chose that one. As we strolled, I realized how the foliage along the fence was so thick that the sidewalk outside was invisible. The heavy greenery by the fence muffled the noise of traffic, and it seemed as if we were far away from the city. The only sounds were the chirping of birds and the distant wailing of the little boy back at the fountain.

When the path veered to the left, I knew our house must be somewhere on the other side of the fence and sidewalk. Here the wooded area was dense with trees and shrubbery, and to get close to the fence, I had to shove my way through branches and vegetation. I had worn my new black shorts, and the twigs and plants scratched my bare legs.

Why would anyone climb through this thicket to look out at our house? Perhaps they wanted to use the bushes for a toilet. Yuk. There would be no need to do that. There were restrooms near the entrance.

I reached an area deep in the woods that seemed likely

to be opposite my house. As I pulled the brush away, I noticed some shrubs and small trees had broken branches. I bent down and found shoe prints in the damp soil. They were large—like men's shoes. Yes, someone had been here. I did not imagine it.

Directly across the street, my house was as clear as could be. Frieda was distinctly visible, collecting the breakfast dishes from the patio table. The French doors to the library still had the curtains pulled from last night. Everything seemed so close, I knew that with the drapes open and the lights on, anyone in the library or dining room could easily be seen from this spot. There was no other reason for anyone to come to this place, except to watch our house.

It was obvious that Adrie was a German agent, even though she did not tell me in so many words. Why else would her boss be the head of *Abwehr*—intelligence? We fled Maine because she was about to be captured—and the U-boat was waiting for us. I could understand that while we were in Maine, someone might be watching her, suspecting that she was a German agent. However, who would be spying on her here in Germany?

Adrie wasn't a bit worried when I told her I saw someone out here. Maybe seeing the watcher in the park meant nothing, just as she had said.

"Perhaps I should forget the whole thing," I whispered to Watcher.

Once again I recalled the shadow—the outline of someone who was looking straight at me.

No, I would bet my last dime that this person had some reason to be watching our house. I looked down at the footprints again, and a chill came over me, raising the hair on my arms. But the big question was: *Is that person watching Adrie—or me?*

11
Barret

Watcher and I scrambled out of the thicket and back onto the paved trail. We continued to circle the park until we arrived at the entrance again from the other side.

I was about to leave, and was turning the corner, when a young man who looked to be about seventeen came from the other direction and almost bumped into us. The dog he held by a harness stopped suddenly, avoiding a near collision.

"Entschuldigen Sie bitte," he said in German.

I recognized the word for "apology," but finding it difficult to say, I answered in English. "I'm sorry."

I couldn't help noticing how good-looking he was, even with the dark glasses shielding his eyes. The brown-and-black German shepherd guide dog stood alert, as if at attention. This dog wore a harness with a handle, but it also had a beautiful leather collar decorated with large colored glass stones.

"Pretty boy!" I murmured. The dog tilted its head and watched me cautiously.

"She's a female." The young man surprised me by replying in English—with a slight German accent. "Her name is Heidi."

"She is beautiful . . . *schön*," I said.

He smiled, nodded, and fondled the dog's ears. It was easy to see how much he loved his dog.

"You speak English," I said. "I'm surprised to meet someone who speaks my language. In fact, I can spot a British accent there."

"You are right. I went to school for many years in England. At a school for the blind."

"And is Heidi your guide dog?" I asked. "I can see how well trained she is. I've heard about guide dogs, but I've never seen one."

"They were first trained here in Germany for veterans who were blinded by gas during the Great War. Now they are used around the world," he told me.

"My dog here is a shepherd too. But of course, he is still just a puppy."

The young man reached down, feeling for Watcher, who went right to his hand and lapped it. I could see him feel my dog's floppy ear. I noticed how Heidi's ears stood up proudly. "His name is Watcher. He's smart, courageous, and very beautiful. He was trained by the SS."

"Should I be afraid of him?"

"No." I laughed. "He failed at military school. He's totally harmless and would probably run in another direction if he were challenged."

"I can tell he's too friendly to be a guard dog for the SS." The young man reached out his hand to me. "I am Barret Hartmann," he said. "And you are . . ."

"I'm Wendy," I replied, shaking his hand. "Wendy Dekker."

Barret was quiet, as if taking in my name. "Do you live nearby? I mean, I have not met you before, have I? I often walk here."

"I live across the street—on Lindenstrasse. Actually, I just moved in. This is the first time I've been to the park."

Barret didn't speak—it was as if he were stunned or not interested at all. It was difficult to speculate what a person might be thinking when he wears dark glasses.

"Well, it's nice to meet you, Barret," I finally said after a moment. "Perhaps I'll bump into you again one of these days."

"I hope so, Wendy. I often walk here, so please say hello when we meet again."

"I will," I assured him.

Barret gave a command at which the dog began to walk again. I watched him as he headed down the sidewalk and crossed the street. I noticed Heidi waited until there was no traffic.

Barret seemed so very nice and gentle and handsome—and he spoke English, too! *I would love to see him again,* I thought. *Maybe we could be friends.*

12
Volunteer Assignment

I hardly noticed the ten or fifteen minutes it took for Watcher and me to head back home, I was so happy to have met Barret. He said he hoped we would meet again. I could hardly wait to tell Adrie that I had a friend—at last!

I looked for Adrie when I arrived, and I found her in the den, on the telephone. She motioned me to a chair, so I sat down with Watcher at my feet while she talked. When I heard her say my name, I tried to decipher what she was saying, but she spoke too fast and there were very few German words that I could catch.

I did notice, though, the intensity of her voice—was she angry? Then she seemed calm and placating—as if she were making peace with whomever was on the line with her.

When she hung up, she was thoughtful and quiet.

"Is everything all right?" I asked.

She looked at me, almost as if she had forgotten I was there. "That was Dr. Ernst—Gertrude's mother. You met them at the tea we went to the other day."

"Oh, yes. Gertrude. You never told me what she said when you introduced us. Remember, how she rattled off?"

"She was rude, and her mother was terribly embarrassed. At any rate, this might be of interest to you. Dr. Ernst, her mother, is the pediatrician at the local Lebensborn center. She wondered if you would like to be a volunteer. I told her you were apprehensive about joining the German Maidens—especially since you speak only English. She thought this might be a good alternative until you learned German and got to know other girls."

"Why me?"

Adrie looked uncomfortable. "Actually, Gertrude wanted the vacancy when and if it came up. However, Dr. Ernst was so put out by her attitude at the tea that she decided, as a punishment to Gertrude, you should have this position if you want it."

"In other words, she's offering me this volunteer assignment to punish Gertrude?"

Adrie raised her eyebrows. "Um, yes."

"Now Gertrude will hate me even more! And, by the way, I never did hear what she said that day."

"You don't want to."

"Yes, I do."

"It was just a tirade about you being American and perhaps not trustworthy. We are at war, Wendy. She is not a happy person to start with—and she is certainly not as pretty as you are. It's jealousy, of course. Here you are, as pretty as a picture—and she assumes you are American. She noticed how everyone greeted you sweetly. That was even more reason for her to be envious, just like those girls in Maine. It all boils down to resentment and envy."

"She never even got to know me." I felt the same way I did in Maine, when the girls there were so cruel. Now, if I took that volunteer job at Lebensborn, I was certain Gertrude and her friend Rikka would get back at me somehow.

"I think you'd like working at Lebensborn," Adrie replied.

"I don't even know what Lebensborn is. It doesn't matter anyway because I don't want to volunteer there."

Adrie drew herself up tall. "Oh, you can't say no to Dr. Ernst. She would be incensed."

"Well, too bad. I thought this was a volunteer job. No one asked me if I wanted to do it."

I could see Adrie's anger beginning to flare. "You didn't want to go to the youth group. You whined about your inability to speak German. You are afraid of the girls. Well, get over it! You've got this opportunity, and you will take it." She got up and headed out of the room.

"Shouldn't that be my decision?" I called out.

Adrie whirled around. "No. It's my decision," she snapped. "And you'll start next week."

13
At the Lebensborn Nursery

Adrie made an appointment for me at the Lebensborn nursery in Berlin for the following week. At first I was angry that I had no choice in the matter, but the more I thought about it, I decided it would be better to take care of babies and little children at the Lebensborn nurseries than to be miserable with a bunch of girls who didn't want to know me anyway.

"Where do the Lebensborn babies and children come from?" I asked Adrie.

"Oh, many of the children are homeless or from other countries—Czechoslovakia and Poland; wherever SS officers find healthy, blond Aryan children without parents. Then they're brought back here for a new life as German children."

"What happened to their real parents?"

Adrie hesitated for a moment then said, "I don't know.

What does it matter? The children will have a better future here."

"So Lebensborn is like an orphanage?"

"In a way. If a German family wants to, they can apply to adopt these homeless children. But that family must prove it is Aryan and German for several generations back. We are nurturing a new world, remember."

"I think it would be wrong to steal children from one country and bring them to another." Then I asked, "What about the babies? Are they from other countries too?"

"No, these babies were born of SS officers and beautiful Aryan German women."

"Are their parents married?"

"Don't ask so many questions." Adrie shook her head, as if exasperated. "You'll find out more about it after you've been here awhile."

Now the day had come when I would begin my work at the Lebensborn. As Adrie and I, in the new Opel, pulled in to a parking space in front of the Lebensborn, I peered out to see a cold-looking gray stone building. "This looks too dreary to be a children's residence."

"It was a private residence before Herr Himmler felt we needed a Lebensborn home here in Berlin."

A large flag flew from the side of the building. It didn't contain a swastika, but it had two strange letters that resembled the *SS*.

"What is that?" I asked, pointing to the flag.

"It's an ancient runic letter that stands for the SS. They

represent a flash of lightning. The children here are protected by the SS," Adrie explained. "No one can ever harm Lebensborn children. Herr Himmler considers them special children because they belong to Germany."

As we headed for the front door, we passed a girl about my age who stood on the sidewalk with a money box. When she saw us, she approached and spoke to Adrie in German. Adrie stopped, pulled out money, and tucked it into the box.

"What did she want?" I whispered to Adrie.

"She's begging for money so she can buy a uniform and join the BDM—the *Bund Deutscher Mädel*."

"Speak in English, please."

"It's the Band of German Girls—the Nazi association for girls," Adrie said. "You see, Wendy, the girls here are enthusiastic to join—but not you! You should be as eager."

"I may join, once I learn German."

I followed Adrie up the steps, where she pushed a doorbell. While we waited, I fidgeted anxiously. "I am so nervous. I don't know what to expect or what they expect of me."

"You'll be fine. It's only three days a week, and I can bring you and pick you up, since I will be working in Berlin anyway. You'll be coming on Mondays, Wednesdays, and Fridays, I was told."

"Why did they ask me to start on a Friday?"

"So you'll have the weekend off to think about things, I suppose."

I shuffled my feet, getting more nervous by the minute.

"Did you tell these people we'd be here today?"

Adrie looked at her watch. "They know you're coming at ten o'clock, and we're right on time."

Just then, the heavy wooden door swung open. "Ah, *guten Morgen*!" A tall, stout woman filled the doorway and greeted us. She stepped back, beckoning us in. "*Ich bin Frau Messner.*"

Frau Messner led us into a large playroom. Toy train tracks with a wooden train and engine big enough for a child to ride wound through the center of the room. Several children played quietly with blocks and playthings scattered about.

One girl, who looked about three years old, was swinging back and forth on a white rocking horse, while a little blond boy stood by crying.

"I think he wants a turn on the rocking horse," I said.

When Adrie translated, Frau Messner called out to the girl, scolding her.

At Frau Messner's tone of voice, the girl climbed off the rocking horse and ran into another room. Yet, instead of taking his turn, the toddler's cries turned into screams and he ran behind a chair.

Frau Messner spoke up quickly and Adrie translated. "'That's little Hunfrid. He's been brought to us from Poland."

"So he's an orphan?" I asked, then waited for Adrie to translate.

"*Ja.*" Frau Messner nodded and explained something to Adrie.

"His parents are dead," Adrie told me. "He is such a perfect little Aryan child, the SS brought him here and named him Hunfrid."

Frau Messner said something else, and Adrie raised her eyebrows. For a moment she paused before telling me what was said. "Um, he is so unhappy and so difficult that they may send him . . . somewhere else. So don't get too fond of him."

"Where is somewhere else?" I asked.

"I don't know," Adrie answered with a frown. "There are other children here who need your help, Wendy. Don't focus on one child."

I picked up a little teddy bear and went over to Hunfrid, who crouched behind a chair.

"Komm zu mir," I said softly, hoping he understood the little German I knew. Instead he squatted down and hid his head.

"Come on out and see me," I said in English in a squeaky voice. But I noticed he was peeking at me from under his arms. I held the bear around the corner of the chair as if it were a puppet, peering at Hunfrid.

"Nein!" He obviously knew the German word for no.

I held the bear's arm, throwing a kiss, and spoke in English. "Come give me a hug, Hunfrid."

"Nein!"

"Ohhh, Hunfrid, *komm zu mir,"* I whined as if the bear were crying. "Hunfrid," I cried.

"Dobry," Hunfrid said suddenly, pointing to himself. "Dobry."

Frau Messner came closer and whispered to Adrie, who then explained to me that Dobry was his Polish name. "You must use only his German name, Hunfrid."

That name would make anyone miserable, I wanted to say. Instead I held the teddy bear close and kissed it on the cheek. "Hunfrid want a kiss too?" I asked, holding the little bear out to him.

The little boy took a step toward me but then looked fearfully at Frau Messner and hid himself again.

Frau Messner spoke brusquely in German, and Adrie translated hesitantly, "Frau says the boy is an obstinate child. He doesn't adapt well." Adrie turned to the supervisor and conversed with her for a few minutes.

That's what they said about Watcher, and they were going to shoot him. I wonder what would happen to this little boy if they sent him to . . . somewhere else.

Finally, Frau Messner nodded and smiled slightly. *"Ja, das ist gut."*

Adrie interpreted the conversation. "I pointed out how well you spoke to Hunfrid even though you primarily speak English. He doesn't speak German either. Frau Messner agreed and said if you'd like to work with him and simply make him comfortable here, that would be fine. He needs to forget his family in Poland. That's why you must teach him that his name is now Hunfrid—not Dobry—and that he's a German boy." Adrie smiled at me. "I think you can do that."

Just then a door on the other side of the playroom opened and a pretty girl—who seemed to be about my age—came across the room. The thick blond braids that wound around her head reminded me of a golden crown, or perhaps a halo. She wore a faded but clean and pressed German dress with the traditional apron.

"Guten Morgen," the girl said. Then, after a few words with Frau Messner, she turned to me. "I am happy to meet you, Wendy. I hope you can understand the little English that I speak. My name is Johanna. We . . . you and I . . . will work together." Smiling, she took ahold of my hands and squeezed them.

At last! A girl my age who is sweet and friendly. And not only that . . . she speaks English!

14
Johanna

"I'll leave you now with Frau Messner and Johanna," Adrie said. "They'll show you around and help you get acquainted with what you'll be doing here."

"As long as I have someone who speaks English, I'll be fine." I turned to Johanna. "Since we'll be working together, maybe you can help me with my German."

"I'll be happy to help you, Wendy. And you can correct me with my English."

"You speak English very well," I assured her. "Where did you learn it?"

"In school. I was in a special school for advanced students—until I was expelled."

I was surprised to hear she was expelled from school! She seemed so poised and intelligent. "I notice you pronounced my name properly."

"It is difficult for Germans to pronounce *w* and *j*. You

probably noticed, my name is spelled with the letter *j* but pronounced as a *y*. Yo-hanna."

Before Adrie left, she beckoned to me as she stood by the door. "Wendy," she whispered when I went to her. "Don't get too friendly with that girl Johanna. She is not here for the same reason as you are. Frau Messner said she has been assigned to Lebensborn for reeducation, to change her ways. They have been unable to do anything with her. She is a bright, intelligent girl, but she has been obstinate and a traitor to the Fatherland. She had better change soon, or . . . well, her family is already in the camps."

"Camps? What kind of camps?"

"Work camps—rehabilitation camps."

I slowly remembered hearing about concentration camps where people were sent who did not cooperate with the Nazis. "She said she had been expelled from her school. Why? What has she or her family done?"

"She's a *Bibelforscher*—one of those International Bible Students who will not capitulate and renounce their religion. She will not salute our Führer, and she considers herself neutral in this war."

"I don't care whether she's a *Bibel* . . . whatever . . . or not," I argued. "I could use a friend my own age."

Adrie sighed. "It's all right to work with her, but you should never be friends. Frau Messner seems to like and respect her. But Johanna had better yield her beliefs or . . ."

"Or what? She'll be sent away to the camps too?"

"Most likely." Adrie walked out the door.

I went back to Johanna, who stood waiting for me.

"Where would you like to start, Wendy?" she asked.

"With little Hunfrid over there behind the chair." Once again I crossed over to the little boy who sat on the floor, his thumb in his mouth, looking totally lost and sad. I walked as far as I dared so as not to frighten him into hiding somewhere else. Then I again gathered the fuzzy toy bear in my arms and sat it on the rocking horse. "I don't know children's songs in German," I whispered to Johanna. "But maybe it doesn't matter."

Johanna nodded. "Just a melody and rhythm will delight him. That would be good for your first day."

"We can name the bear Dobry, can't we?"

Johanna hesitated for a moment. "The officers here are very firm and determined to Germanize him." Then she shrugged. "Well, no one is here but us, and it's only the bear that has a Polish name. So I think it will be all right."

I held the bear up and asked, "Want to play, Dobry? Want to go to Boston?" I bounced the teddy bear in my lap as I sang in English a rhyme I had loved as a child.

"Trot, trot to Boston? Trot, trot to Lynn.
Look out, little Dobry, or you might fall . . . IN!"

At the word *in*, I let the bear drop to the floor. I repeated the nursery rhyme several times, waiting for a reaction from Hunfrid. The first few times he only watched, but gradually he showed an interest and even began to laugh when the bear fell "in."

Finally I put my arms out to him. "Want to go to Boston?"

Johanna gasped when Hunfrid climbed onto my lap.

Once again I sang.

"Trot, trot to Boston? Trot, trot to Lynn.
Look out, little Hunfrid, or you might fall . . . IN!"

I let Hunfrid fall holding his hands as he dropped to keep him from falling to the floor. Soon he was laughing and wanting more.

"Więcej."

"That must mean 'more' in Polish," Johanna said, looking concerned. "We need to teach him how to say *more* in German, or Frau will be angry." She clapped her hands to get Hunfrid's attention. *"Mehr! Mehr!"* she said.

Hunfrid became still for a moment. Then he yelled, "*Mehr. Mehr.*"

"Gut! Gut!" Johanna pulled a cookie from her apron pocket and gave it to him.

"Gut!" exclaimed Hunfrid as he bit into the cookie. Then he looked up at me. *"Mehr,"* he said. "Boston."

Within a short time, I sang quiet songs and rocked Hunfrid as I sang. Soon he had fallen asleep in my arms. His blond hair clung around his forehead, and his adorable face melted my heart. This baby was so lost. How did his parents die? Why did the SS bring him here to Berlin? Surely, he must have had other relatives back in Poland who were worried about him and would take him.

Frau Messner came by with a nod and a smile of approval, and I gave Hunfrid a kiss on his cheek before she took him from me to another room.

After lunch in the children's dining hall, Johanna showed me around the nursery where the newborns and youngest babies lived. I had never seen so many babies at once. The changing table was huge and covered with thick leather padding and filled with dozens of wiggling babies. Nursemaids in uniforms stuffed bottles and pacifiers into their mouths; others changed diapers, rocked, walked, soothed screams, sang songs . . . The sounds, noises, and commotion reminded me of a zoo rather than a nursery.

Suddenly nurses shoved two babies each into our arms and gave orders in German.

"They've been fed and now they want us to rock them to sleep," Johanna explained.

"Where are their mothers?"

"Some are upstairs getting well after the births—others are gone now."

"Will they be back? Don't they want their babies?"

"Some work here so they can be near their babies. However, the babies are no longer theirs. These babies belong to the SS and are under its protection."

The babies howled and wiggled, and I held on to them tightly for fear they would squirm right out of my arms. "They'll never go to sleep with so much noise in here."

"They're used to noise." Johanna pointed to rocking chairs near the windows. Then we both sat and rocked as we held the babies close. Johanna sang a lullaby. She had a sweet voice, and the babies quieted down with her song. It was nice and comfortable holding them. They were soft and warm, newly bathed, and smelled of fresh soap and baby powder. It wasn't long before all four of them were asleep.

"How long have you been volunteering here?" I asked Johanna as we tucked the babies into bassinets.

"For over a year now." Johanna looked at me with a sad smile. "I'm really not a volunteer. I'm here for the same reason as little Hunfrid out there in the other room. They are trying to make me become one of them too—a loyal Nazi."

"I . . . don't understand. You aren't Polish like Hunfrid, are you?"

"No, I'm German," Johanna said softly as she smoothed the babies' blankets. "They . . . the *Reich* . . . the government wants to change my thinking—things I've been brought up to believe that make me who I am. We no longer have freedom of religion. Because I speak German, French, and English, they feel I would be valuable to them. So they put me here instead of the camps. All the while, they try to convince me to give up my beliefs. But my parents and my brother are already in the camps because they would never disown our God." Before she looked away, I could see her eyes brighten with tears. "I miss them, and I worry so much about them."

"The camps don't seem so bad," I said, trying to make her feel better. "I've seen newsreels where detainees were having a nice time dancing and playing musical instruments. They're being treated well, aren't they?"

Johanna leaned close to me and whispered. "What you

see in the newsreels is not what is really happening in the camps. It is not true."

"I don't understand. . . ."

"You will—eventually."

"Why is your family in concentration camps, Johanna? They're not criminals—and they're German, aren't they?"

Johanna frowned. "We will not 'Heil Hitler,' for one thing."

"Why not?" I asked.

"Maybe you don't realize it, but the word *Heil* in German means . . . um . . . 'salvation' in English. I cannot salute Hitler as if he is God. All we Bible Students live good lives and obey the law. All we ask for is freedom to practice and live our religion. But they—the Nazis—are determined that *Bibelforscher* should renounce our religion or we will be put in the camps—even put to death."

"What? Put to death?" I could not imagine such a thing. "You must be mistaken."

"Wendy, you have no idea how many . . . undesirables . . . Jews, Gypsies, *Bibelforscher*—are disappearing once they're put into the camps, even if they are German."

"There must be something you can do to avoid that."

"*Ja.* They have given *Bibelforscher* a choice because we are German citizens. If we sign a paper saying we will give up our religion and Heil Hitler and obey the Nazi rules, we can go free."

"You mean if you just sign a paper, you'll be free?"

Johanna nodded.

"That seems easy enough," I said after thinking about

this for a moment. "Why not just sign the paper, and then do what you want?"

"I couldn't live with myself if I did that. You don't understand." She stood up to leave. "I've said too much already."

I grabbed ahold of her sleeve as she started to walk away. "Please don't go, Johanna. I'm sorry. You're right. I don't understand. And trust me, I'm here only because I have to volunteer at something, not to spy on you."

Johanna swung around, and I could tell she was not convinced. "I hope not."

"I'm here because I didn't want to join the girls' youth groups." I lowered my voice. "They don't seem to be doing anything useful. They dance around and do cartwheels and wave flags—at least that's what I've heard and seen in the newspapers. And what's worse—they're only my age, and I've heard many of them are being groomed to be mothers."

"*Ja*, most of the babies here have young, unmarried mothers," Johanna said with a nod. "But the children will probably never live with them."

"Well, I certainly don't want to be a young unmarried mother. I would much rather be here just caring for the babies. That's why Dr. Ernst asked me to . . ."

Johanna took in a breath and her eyes widened. "You are friends with Dr. Ernst?"

"I only met her . . ."

"I didn't realize you . . . " Johanna straightened her apron and then turned to walk away. "I can't help you after all." This time she moved quickly and resolutely away from me.

"Why not?" I called after her. "What have I done?"

Johanna whirled around accusingly. "She—Dr. Ernst and her daughter, Gertrude—put you here to . . . trap me . . . to make me surrender who I am inside." She patted her chest. "To make me one of them." She stood tall, her face determined.

"I hardly know them. In fact, Gertrude was so rude to me, her mother gave me this job instead of her. She would be here in my place if she could be. Neither of them is a friend of mine," I said, crossing the room to catch up with her. I put my hand on Johanna's arm. "Please don't go. Can't we be friends and work together?"

Johanna stared at me for a moment and must have seen the earnest sadness I was feeling, because she reached out to me. "I would like a friend, but only someone I can trust. You tell me to sign the paper and be free. I would rather you encourage me to stand firm in what I believe. That's what a friend would do." Her voice quavered.

"I'm sorry, Johanna. Where I come from we never hear of things like this. We aren't given choices like this. I think you are very brave."

Johanna came closer and whispered again. "Anything I say might endanger my family or my friends. If you are a friend of Dr. Ernst, or . . ."

"I swear to you, I hardly know either of them."

"I want to believe you, Wendy," she said with a cautious smile.

I put out my hand, pleading. "Please believe me."

Johanna took my hand. "We will be friends, but please, don't try to talk me out of my Christian decision. And don't ever betray my trust."

"Never," I promised.

I spent the rest of the day working with Johanna. Little Hunfrid followed me around—grabbing my skirt, wanting to be bounced or just held. He carried the little teddy bear Dobry close to him wherever he went.

By the time I was ready to leave in the late afternoon, Hunfrid had learned my name. "Wen-dee! Wen . . . dee!" he called after me whenever I went out of his sight. I gave him a hug, and a kiss on the cheek, when I saw Adrie's car outside. Immediately he knew I was leaving and began to cry.

I could hear his sobs as I ran out the door to the driveway. Johanna held Hunfrid up to the window to wave good-bye. However, Hunfrid cried and held his arms out as if calling me to come back.

"I hate to leave him. I feel like I should go back and hold him," I said to Adrie.

"He needs to know you won't be here all the time. As I said, do not become too attached, or you will be the one to get hurt. You heard Frau Messner. She said he might be sent somewhere else."

"Where? Tell me. Where is somewhere else?"

"I don't know. Perhaps he'll be put up for adoption."

Even though adoption would be better than living in the Lebensborn, something about Adrie's answer did not ring true. Where would they send little Hunfrid, really?

A sinking feeling surged over me as I remembered what the SS officer said about Watcher. *He's worthless and can't be trained. We'll have to put him down.*

What might happen to Hunfrid and Johanna if they "couldn't be trained"? Were they considered worthless? Would they be put down?

Of course not!

Don't be foolish, I told myself.

15
The Watcher from the Woods

Having Watcher jump up and lap my face when I got home from the Lebensborn helped me turn off the picture in my head of little Hunfrid with his arms outstretched to me.

After supper Adrie went to her office and turned on the radio to hear the news. Frieda was busy tidying up and bringing in clothing from the closed-in yard on the other side of the house, where she hung the laundry.

Out of curiosity, before the darkness of night set in, I went to the library and stood by the patio door. The leaves of the park were still. I wondered if I would ever see the watcher in the woods again. Then I remembered Barret! I had been so overwhelmed with Adrie, the new car, the puppy, and that awful tea party, I had forgotten all about Barret.

It was just as well I hadn't mentioned Barret to Adrie. If

I had, Adrie would probably have forbidden me to see him again. Look how concerned she was about Johanna.

Don't make friends with her, she had said. She even warned me not to get attached to little Hunfrid.

I was sure now that if I ever did see Barret again, I would keep our friendship to myself.

I decided to take a walk in the cool evening air. I knew I should ask permission, so Watcher and I went to the den where Adrie was sitting close to the radio, her face serious. She put her finger to her lips. "Sh! There's an announcement." I waited while the announcer spoke in a loud, excited voice.

Adrie turned the volume down. "The sixth army is battling with the Russians. To win Stalingrad will be a tough battle. I hope they can take the city before winter comes." Adrie looked worried. Then, turning to me she asked, "Did you want something?"

"Yes. I'm going for a walk with Watcher."

"Go for your walk, but be back here before dark." Adrie fiddled with the radio. "I'm going to see if I can get England and hear what lies they're telling now." She turned the volume back up.

"Come along with me, Watcher."

Watcher wiggled and hopped around, then ran to the hooks where his leash hung.

"You are such a smart puppy! You remember where I keep your leash!" I clicked the hook onto my dog's collar, and he danced around me, tangling my legs in the leash. "Calm down, Watcher," I said, laughing.

I decided to take a shortcut to the sidewalk behind the house, so we went out to the terrace and down a seldom-used set of stairs to the back wooden gate that creaked open onto the street and sidewalk.

We crossed the street and walked along the sidewalk. The scent of climbing roses on the park fence was scattered on the evening breeze. Then the aroma of a pipe flowed through the air. Someone nearby must be smoking, although I did not see anyone around me.

Suddenly I heard German voices drifting from inside the park—on the other side of the iron fence—from the woods where I had seen the silhouette of a man. I paused and strained to hear. Two voices in a soft conversation and the familiar scent of pipe tobacco drifted through the trees.

Watcher stopped, his head turned, listening. He gave one quick bark, and I put my hand on his head. "Sh, Watcher," I whispered. Watcher stopped barking and stood alert, except for that one floppy ear. I noticed that when I spoke in whispers, Watcher often became still, as if he knew he must not bark or move.

The voices stopped. I tried not to gaze in their direction, although I could tell they were near the fence. I started walking again, as if I had heard nothing. Once we passed the corner, we ran down the sidewalk toward the park gate.

"I've got to see who's in there before they have a chance to leave," I told myself breathlessly. As I turned to go through the entrance, I looked up to see an elderly man and a youth with a dog coming down the outer pathway.

The older man was smoking a pipe. I took in a breath as I recognized the young man with him. "Barret!" I didn't mean to say his name aloud, but I was surprised to see him there.

The two men stopped in surprise and the dog, Heidi, stood still, her eyes on Watcher and me. "Who is it?" Barret asked.

"It's me. Wendy."

The older man grasped Barret's arm, and an expression of alarm and astonishment passed over his face.

Watcher stood close and began to bark loudly. "It's all right, Watcher," I said, patting his head and ears. "Sit! I mean, *sitz*!" Watcher looked up at me quizzically and then sat at my feet.

"So, this is the wonderful dog you told me about," Barret said slowly. "I can tell he's well trained—and he speaks German." A smile broke over his face.

The old man said nothing, but eyed me curiously.

"I . . . I'm sorry if I startled you," I apologized, and wondered if the man spoke English too. "Barret and I seem to be bumping into each other lately." I turned to Barret. "Do you live nearby, Barret?"

"Not too far away," he replied. "My grandfather and I come here to walk the dog." Barret gestured toward the older man, who still held on to Barret's arm. "May I introduce my grandfather Konrad Strohkirch? I'm sorry, but I am not sure of your full name, Wendy."

"Wendy Dekker." I noticed Herr Strohkirch's eyes widen again when I said my name. "Have we met before, sir?"

"No, I don't believe so, but I did know your father," Herr Strohkirch answered. "I have wanted to meet you for a very long time." He looked at me closely. "Oh my, you resemble your mother." He gestured to one of the park benches by the pool. "Please sit down with us here."

A sudden chill ran up my spine. Who really was this man who knew my name and was so eager to meet me?

Then I knew—this was the watcher from the woods.

16
Herr Konrad Strohkirch

The sun was sinking rapidly behind the trees as I studied the elderly man. Could this harmless-looking old man, Barret's grandfather, be the fearful shadow I had seen among the trees? Heidi and Watcher sat at his feet, their tails wagging lazily as he stroked their heads.

Nevertheless, if it was him, why had he lurked among the foliage, watching our house—watching me? I needed to know.

"I can see you're bewildered," Herr Strohkirch said. "As I said, I am an old friend of your father's."

Barret reached out and touched his grandfather's arm. "Are we visible from the entrance?"

"*Ja.* We must move farther back in the park," Herr Strohkirch agreed. "In case Adrie—"

"No. If you have something to say, please tell me now." I would not be led back into the shadowy paths of the park with this stranger, no matter how kind he seemed. "I am not going anywhere with someone who stood in the bushes spying on our house."

"I am sorry if I frightened you," Herr Strohkirch said. "You see, I heard you were coming to Berlin, but I needed to be sure."

"How did you know I was coming? Did Adrie notify you?"

"No, not Adrie, but I was informed. Wendy, you have several people who care for you and are concerned about you." Barret's grandfather leaned back and his eyes searched mine. "I know, seeing you, that you are the young woman I've been waiting for—for many years, my child." He paused and smiled. "You look so much like your mother, but you have your father's blue eyes."

"My father had brown eyes."

"Oh, your father had eyes as blue as the sky," Herr Strohkirch said with certainty.

His gaze went to the ruby ring on my right hand. I warily pushed it into my pocket. Was my valuable ring the reason for this encounter?

"Your father gave that ring to Adrie. It is a pigeon-blood ruby. This is even more proof that you are the one for whom I've waited to fulfill your father's request."

"My father and I never knew each other."

"That is true. However, he wanted you to know him and he wanted to protect you. I promised him before he died that I would contact you when you were older and if you came back to your home in Germany—"

“Opa, knowing the truth might put Wendy in danger,” Barret cut in.

“I also promised her father to keep her safe,” Herr Strohkirch replied.

The evening shadows were deepening, and I knew Adrie would be upset if I didn’t get back soon. “Why don’t both of you come to the house with me and you can speak with my mother? I’m sure she would be pleased to meet you, especially if you are a friend of my father’s.” I glanced at Barret, who looked uncomfortable as he patted his dog.

Herr Strohkirch frowned. “Wendy, your mother would never let me see you. She would be angry if she knew we met.”

I felt muddled. If Adrie was so cautious that I must not meet Herr Strohkirch, perhaps I shouldn’t stay and listen to what he had to tell me. Yet, at the same time, if Adrie did not want me to meet Herr Strohkirch, she would not want me to be friends with Barret, either. And I really liked Barret.

“I must go,” I said, standing up. “Adrie will be furious if I don’t get home before dark.”

“Yes, Adrie has a strong will,” Herr Strohkirch said. “Your father was the opposite—a kind, gentle man. He was not the man you think he was.”

“Not the man I think? I don’t understand.”

“*Ach, mein Kind.* This is not the time or place for you to grasp all I have to tell you. We need more time to talk. I must ask a favor, Wendy. Please do not mention our . . . er . . .

coincidental . . . meeting to your mother. Keep this between us for now—for your father's sake."

"I don't like to keep things from Adrie."

"Please trust me. You have every right to know the things I have to tell you about your wonderful father—things that have been kept from you. I am sure Adrie has hidden away pieces of your background that are awaiting you in that house. Listen to your heart. Then, when you are ready, we will meet again."

I headed for the front gate, realizing the sun had set and the park was empty except for the three of us. "How can I get in touch with you, if I decide to hear what you have to say?"

"I often walk to this park with my dog," Barret said. "We will meet again . . . won't we?"

I felt my face redden. I wanted to meet Barret again. Besides, I did want to know more about my father. Still . . . I wasn't sure.

"When you are ready to hear what I have to say, you will find us, or we will find you," Herr Strohkirch said. "Next time we are together, I will tell you all about your father. However, do not mention to Adrie—or to anyone—that you met me. If you do, you will never know the truth."

"I won't tell anyone," I promised.

17
Unhappy Sunday

This had been a terrible, horrible Sunday morning. Adrie and I had our first real fight. I'm still angry every time I think about it.

After breakfast I decided to look up Lebensborn in Adrie's library. It was dark in the room, as the air-raid drapes were still drawn. As I went to open them, I grabbed the gold-tasseled cord and yanked it. This time, however, the drapes didn't open. I turned on the desk light and tried to see why the pull cords weren't working.

Had I broken something? I didn't want Adrie to be angry with me. I turned on the overhead lights and saw a twist at the top of the curtain where the cord must have become tangled.

I needed something to stand on so I could reach the top of the French doors and straighten the cord. I pulled the heavy desk chair to the door, but it caught on the

Oriental rug. The chair was too heavy to lift, so I dragged it back and smoothed the carpet.

Then I remembered Adrie saying there was a tall library ladder in the closet. Had she said it was broken? Or had she just said I shouldn't use it to take books down from the top shelf? I couldn't remember, but I didn't want Adrie to discover I had pulled the drapery cord too hard or broken something on the pull cord, so I decided to try the ladder anyway.

I found the ladder tucked away in the corner of the closet. I rolled it out into the room and examined it. It seemed to work fine. I found a knob that tightened the wheels so they'd lock while a person climbed or was searching for books. Perfect!

At that exact moment Adrie entered the room. "What are you doing with that ladder? Didn't I tell you it was broken and not to use it?"

"But it's not broken . . . look." I tried to show her how well the wheels turned.

Adrie's voice was icy and her eyes narrowed. "I requested that you do not climb up to the top shelves of the bookcases. You are not to touch those books. That's all I asked. But here you are, disobeying me."

I had never seen Adrie so mad. "I wasn't going up to the bookshelves. I was trying to fix the drapery cord," I explained. "I'm sorry, but I must have tangled the cord to open them. . . ." My voice cracked. "I was . . . trying to fix them before . . . you found out because I knew you'd be . . . mean . . . just the way you are being right now!" I ran out of the library before Adrie could see me cry.

I heard footsteps behind me and hoped for a moment that they were Adrie's. However, it was Watcher who followed me.

I flew up the long winding stairway to my room, let my puppy in, and then closed the door. I threw myself onto the bed, and Watcher jumped up with me, whining, as if asking what was wrong. I put my arms around him and snuggled my face into his bristly fur. Why was Adrie so angry? Nothing bad happened. I didn't fall. Besides, the ladder wasn't broken. She lied to me. Why?

After a few minutes I lay on my back and looked up at the ceiling. "Adrie breaks my heart when she's like this," I told Watcher. "She's more than mean; she's downright nasty! I should have stayed back in the States—back with Mom and Daddy. Only now I know they aren't my mom and daddy, and since I've come here without calling them, they probably don't love me either. I don't have anyone anymore . . . except you, my sweet little dog." I burst into tears again.

Before long Adrie knocked on the door and peeked in. "Wendy?"

I didn't answer, and buried my face again in Watcher's fur.

"May I come in?"

When I still didn't answer, Adrie entered and sat on the side of the bed. "Wendy, I'm sorry I responded as I did. Can you forgive me?"

I wasn't sure I could forgive her. I was too upset and I wanted to go home.

Adrie continued. "It's no excuse, I know, but I have problems that I need to solve and they're on my mind. I shouldn't have taken them out on you."

I wanted to say, *That's right, you shouldn't.* Instead I just nodded and sniffled. Watcher snuggled his head into my neck and licked my tears.

Adrie went on, and she did sound remorseful. "I overreacted when I saw you with the ladder. It's just that . . . um . . . I thought for sure you'd probably fall, and maybe break your leg. I'm not good at being a mother." She touched my shoulder.

I was still angry, so I pulled away. After a moment I asked her, "Did you know I used to wish you really were my mother? I was so happy when you visited me. I wanted to be with you forever, and I always felt so sad when you left me." I sat up and wiped my eyes on my sleeve. "That's why I didn't want to disappoint you when that drapery cord wouldn't work."

"Then we're both sorry and we'll both be fine, right?" Adrie asked with a pleading smile.

"I . . . guess so. I hate it when you scream at me. Mommy—I mean, Aunt Nixie—never screamed at me."

"Did I scream?"

"Well . . . pretty close. Your voice was icy, and you looked like you hated me."

"Well, I don't hate you. I'd never hate you."

"Adrie, why did you send me away to live in America when I was a baby?"

"Oh, it's hard to explain. But, shortly before you were

born, Germany was in the midst of a depression. The armistice at Versailles after the Great War crippled this country. Why, Germany was required to pay for the entire war! There was no money, no jobs, and no hope. Germans were not allowed to fly or build planes or have an army large enough to protect ourselves. So we decided to have you live with my sister, Nixie, in America until things got better here."

"You had me stay in New York for safety, right? Then why now, in the middle of this war, did you bring me here?"

"Yes, we are at war." Adrie nodded. "But now our Führer has made our country strong again. He brought us out of the depression by creating jobs, making highways, and building up the *Wehrmacht*—our armed forces."

Even with all Adrie's explanations, I didn't understand any of it. But I listened as Adrie went on and on.

"We have the greatest scientists in the world. We will soon have rockets that fly themselves to wherever we want them to go."

Adrie's voice rose and her eyes brightened as she continued. "It will be your generation and your children's generation who will rule the next thousand years. I want you to be part of that great future our Führer has planned. And that is why I brought you home." Adrie looked down at her hands. "I did it for you. You'll thank me someday."

I didn't know what to say so I just nodded.

Adrie took a deep breath. "Now, there's one thing I need to stress again. Do not climb up to those top shelves.

The books up there are out-of-bounds for you. They are all in German and . . . nothing you'd be interested in. Do you understand?"

"I wasn't going for the books. I was trying to fix the cord. . . ."

"I know, I know." Adrie stood up and pulled me by my hand. "Let's go down and fix that drapery cord together."

When Adrie, Watcher, and I reached the library, however, Frieda was already on the ladder, untangling the cord. We all laughed as Watcher tried to follow Frieda up the ladder, and then slipped to the floor.

"You silly little dog." I gathered him into my lap. He looked up at me remorsefully and then licked my face. "I love you to pieces," I told him.

When I looked up, I could see Adrie watching us, and I wondered what she was thinking.

You have never told me you love me, I wanted to say.

18

Three Wise Monkeys

Adrie and Frieda surprised me with a party for my fifteenth birthday. Of course it was just Adrie, Frieda, and me—who else did I know who would attend my party? If I were back in Maine, I'd have a real party with Jill—my best friend there, the one who stood by me. And I'd invite Quarry—the boy who lived in the lighthouse. Mom and Daddy would drive up from New York. I wondered what Mom and Daddy were doing today. They were sad, I was sure.

Frieda made a beautiful German chocolate cake, and we ate dinner in the dining room. I was also allowed a small glass of wine. Adrie presented me with a gold charm bracelet. It had three gold monkeys hanging from its links.

"Oh, Adrie, you remembered how I fell in love with Jill's bracelet. And now I have one too." I held out my hand, and Adrie fastened the bracelet on my wrist.

"Yes, I do remember. Her father—that singer—sent it to her while he was on tour, as I recall."

"Her dad is famous! He's on the radio all the time in the States," I reminded her. "But her bracelet was silver, not gold—and it didn't have ruby eyes like these monkeys do."

"I thought the ruby eyes would match your ring. And rubies are your birthstone."

"You always think of everything. Thank you, Adrie."

"Each of these wise monkeys has a lesson to teach." Adrie took my hand and pointed to the first monkey. "This one has his hands over his eyes. That means 'see no evil.' The second has his hands over his ears—'hear no evil.' And the third has his hands over his mouth—see? This advises you to speak no evil." She looked at me with raised eyebrows. "What do you think they are telling you?"

I was silent as I thought about this. Then I answered, "I shouldn't believe everything I hear—or speak about it. And if I see something that is ugly or cruel—I must close my eyes to it."

"*Ja. Gut!* The monkeys warn you that thinking, speaking, or dwelling on negative things—or things you don't understand—can harm you." Adrie patted my hand and stood up. "That is the best advice I can give you."

The following few weeks flew by quickly, and it was near the end of August before I realized it. I went to the park several times, determined to meet with Barret and his grandfather again, but they were never there when I was. I began to wonder if I had dreamed the whole incident of that day in the park.

Meanwhile, I was enjoying my work with the children at Lebensborn. Once, Dr. Ernst had come in with her daughter, Gertrude—along with Gertrude's sidekick, Rikka. I'd avoided them, thanks to Johanna, who hid me in a closet on the third floor. We laughed after they left, feeling satisfied to have outwitted the two wicked stepsisters, as we called them in English (between ourselves).

I loved Johanna. We shared lunchtime together, which was when she helped me to speak German. I found her to be sweet, fun, a caring worker, and soon the dearest friend I ever had anywhere.

When I showed her my bracelet and what it stood for, she was quiet and thoughtful. Then she said, "Do you think that advice—see no evil or hear no evil—is always correct? Sometimes aren't we responsible to open our eyes and see the wickedness and evil in the world and then speak up about it?"

"I hadn't thought about it like that," I answered, suddenly disappointed in myself.

We both loved the children at Lebensborn. Hunfrid, who was my favorite, was getting to be comfortable in his new home. He was speaking some German words and called me "Ven-dee." He called Johanna "Yo-Yo."

Johanna played a small accordion, sang German folk songs to the children, and before long Hunfrid and I were singing them too. One of the favorites was an old German folk song.

Lady-bird! Lady-bird! Pretty one, stay;
Come, sit on my finger, so happy and gay.
With me shall no mischief betide thee.
No harm would I do thee, no foeman is near—
I only would gaze on thy beauties so dear,
These beautiful winglets beside thee.

"That's only the first verse." Johanna gave me a long look then said. "To me, you are the lady-bird."

"How so?"

"You could have stayed in a happy, safe place, but you flew off to Germany."

"No, I sailed off to Germany," I said with a laugh. "Tell us what happens to the lady-bird. Sing us the second verse."

Lady-bird! Lady-bird! Fly away home;
Your house is on fire, your children will roam!
List, list, to their cry and bewailing!
The pitiless spider is weaving their doom!
Then, lady-bird! Lady-bird! Fly away home,
Hark, hark! To thy children's bewailing!

"That's scary. I'm not sure what it means," I said. "If I am the lady-bird, who are the children? And who is the pitiless spider?"

"That's the riddle for you to figure out," Johanna said with a little smile.

I didn't know why the song and its meaning made a nest in my head, but I found myself wondering about it often.

19
Adrie's Plans

I wanted desperately to see Barret and his grandfather. At times I wondered if their story and warnings were just a hoax. But I was still curious how they knew I was in Germany, and why they waited and watched for me. I had to find out.

Therefore, I was pleased when Adrie told me on Friday night that she had to go away on business. She was in her room, packing a suitcase, and called to me.

"Wendy, I have to go to Munich for a while, and I'm hoping you won't go out after dark when I'm gone. You have to maintain your schedule at Lebensborn. Be careful! Promise me that you will stay at home and not go gallivanting off somewhere."

"Where and how and with whom would I go gallivanting?"

"You know what I mean."

"How will I get to Lebensborn?"

"Take a bus. One leaves from the corner of our street on the hour and half hour, and goes almost to the Lebensborn door. Or you can call a taxi. Oh, and by the way, I've called Frau Messner, and she's going to arrange for you to learn German with Johanna on your lunch hours from now on."

"Did you need to get permission? Johanna and I have already been doing it for weeks."

"I wasn't sure how wise it would be for Johanna to be used in that way without permission. After all, she is a . . . detainee. She may be bright, but she is also stupid. All she needs to do as a German citizen is sign her name on a paper and she'd be free."

"I don't think she's stupid. I think she's brave and loyal to what she believes."

"You think she's loyal?" Adrie turned and glared at me. "On second thought, perhaps I should not allow you to spend time with her."

"Oh, I have no idea what Johanna believes—it has nothing at all to do with me," I replied, and quickly changed the subject. "So why must you go to Munich? What if it's bombed?"

"It is an important city and could be a target at some point," Adrie replied. "However, they are prepared with siren warnings and have many shelters everywhere."

"Why are you going?" I was worried for her—and for myself, too. What if something happened to Adrie? I'd be alone in this strange country.

Adrie sat on her bed. "I have to go because . . . there is a resistance group there that is causing trouble."

"Sabotage?" I asked.

"No, although it might lead to that. This is a group of students who print leaflets filled with lies about our Führer. They call themselves the White Rose group."

"What are they saying in the leaflets?"

"Terrible things. 'Every word that comes from Hitler's mouth is a lie,'" Adrie quoted in a sarcastic voice. "'When he says peace, he means war, and when he blasphemously uses the name of the Almighty, he means the power of evil, the fallen angel, Satan.' Imagine! Calling our Führer, Satan! I should not be telling you all this, but since you were worried, I wanted you to understand that I am not in great danger. My job is to find out who the leaders of this gang are." She shut her suitcase. "Everything will be fine."

"I hope so."

"I've left money and bus tokens on my desk. There is a phone number where I might be reached, but only for an emergency, Wendy."

I carried Adrie's overnight bag and her briefcase out to the car, and she took the suitcase. Frieda came running out with a thermos and a brown bag filled with cookies for Adrie's trip. After a few words with Frieda, Adrie climbed into the car and drove off.

That night I found it hard to sleep. There were too many new questions creeping into my thoughts—especially Herr Strohkirch's words: . . . *tucked and hidden away are the memories that Adrie's tried so hard to keep from you . . . and even from herself . . . pieces of your background that are awaiting you in that house. Then, when you are ready, we will meet again.*

I sat up. Since I couldn't sleep anyway, I thought I might as well start my search for whatever it was that Adrie might have hidden from me. The first place I'd check would be that top shelf in the library. There had to be something important up there or Adrie would not have made such a scene. If there was something about my life and my father in those books, I had every right to know.

However, I'd need to be extremely careful. If Adrie found out, I didn't know what she would do.

20
Trapped!

The clock on the table by my bed said one fifteen. Surely, Frieda was asleep by now. I slipped out of bed, peeked out my bedroom door, and found the house silent and dark. After taking a flashlight from my bedside table, I tiptoed down the shadowy hallway to the stairs.

I made my way noiselessly into the library so neither Watcher nor Frieda would hear me. After shutting the library door, I flashed the light on the closet and opened it. Then I carried the heavy ladder to the bookshelves, praying that I would not stumble or drop it. I turned the switches that locked the legs and set the ladder up against the shelves.

Cautiously, I climbed each rung and flashed my light on the leather-bound books on the highest shelf. I stood on the top rung of the ladder, reached up as high as I could, and was able to pull three of the heavy books toward me.

Holding the books under one arm, I climbed down the ladder, set the books on the reading table, and turned on the desk lamp. To my delight and excitement, I discovered two of the books were photograph albums. I chose the third book to examine first, saving the photos until last.

I discovered that the third book contained documents written in German. As I sifted through them, one in English caught my eye. It was my birth certificate from the State of New York—city of Buffalo. There was my name, Wendy Adriane Dekker. Birth Date: July 25, 1927. Mother: Adrie Dekker; Father: Karl Dekker.

Well, that was interesting. Adrie says I am 100 percent German. However, even if my parents are German, I was born in the USA; that makes me American as well!

I wondered if the other documents were important to me, but since they were written in legal-looking German, I put everything back in the book and set it aside.

The pictures in the first album, yellowed with age, were of men and women who I didn't know, dressed in old-fashioned clothing.

Why should these photographs be off-limits? I wondered. I had no idea who these people were. As I reached the back, I found pictures of a smiling baby and the name Adrie written in faded ink. I couldn't help but smile. She was a cute baby who reminded me of me in my own baby pictures back in New York. I wondered if Adrie had any of my pictures here. She must have received pictures of me as I was growing up. I closed the album and set it aside.

The last book was thick with photographs mounted or

stuffed loosely in the pages. When I opened it, photos fell out onto the table and floor. I gathered them together and set them on the tabletop.

My heart skipped as I went over the photos. These were pictures of Adrie and another man. But this man was not my father, Karl Dekker. Who was he? Several pictures were of Adrie and the stranger, sitting on the deck of a big sailboat. Adrie looked dazzling and very young! The man had his arm around her shoulders, and he was looking at her affectionately.

Another photo of that day on the boat was of Adrie and the same man, standing close together. She had her head on his shoulder, and this time he had both his arms around her. Who was he? A friend? No, there was more than friendship in that photograph. There was love in their eyes.

I fumbled my way quickly through the set of pictures. The unfamiliar man was in dozens of them. He sure was handsome, whoever he was. Adrie looked young, shining, and happier than I had ever seen her. In almost every picture where they were together, they clung to each other.

Wait a minute!

In one close-up of Adrie where she held a picnic basket, her hands were clearly in view, and there on her finger was the ruby ring! My father gave her that ruby ring. How could she be flirting and having fun with this stranger, when she was engaged to my father? I was indignant. How could she?

Perhaps this man was a relative. However, Adrie did

not have a brother, and I had never heard of cousins. So who was he? Had she been unfaithful to my father at this time? I turned over each picture to look for dates. Those that were marked had the dates 1924, 1925, and 1926. These pictures were taken before I was born. Yet, clearly, she was engaged to my father at that time because she wore the ruby ring.

I sat back in the chair, confused and puzzled, when suddenly I heard a car coming up our driveway, its lights flashing through the front windows.

It must be Adrie! If she found me in the library with the ladder and the books, she would never forgive me. I turned off the desk lamp and grabbed the books and the loose pictures. *What shall I do with them?* Hastily, I stuffed them into a wastebasket, rushed to the closet, and set the wastebasket inside.

I had no time to put the ladder away. Already I could hear someone unlocking the front door, just outside the library.

It had to be Adrie. Had she seen the light on in the library? I glanced around, looking for a place to hide, and without another thought I went into the closet and silently closed the door.

I heard the front door open and close. The hall light went on, and I could see the crack of light under the door. I heard her in her den, desk drawers opening and shutting. Then I heard her footsteps going up the stairway.

If she looked in my bedroom and found me gone, then what? She would certainly look everywhere, and then she'd find me in here! She'd see the ladder and notice the books on the top shelf were gone.

I couldn't possibly hide the ladder. It was too big and complicated to take it apart quickly, especially in the dark.

I trembled at the thought, and I felt my heart pounding in my chest. I'd have to confess everything and beg her to forgive me.

21
Lies

W*hat shall I do? No time to think!* I tiptoed out into the hall, closed the library door softly, and raced to the kitchen. I shut the kitchen door and turned on the small light over the sink. I was relieved that Watcher was not under the table and was most likely in Frieda's room; otherwise, he would have barked and whined.

After grabbing cookies from a new ceramic cookie jar, I slumped into a chair at the table as if I'd been there for a while. My heart was pounding so furiously, I wondered if it could be heard, and I was gasping for breath as if I'd been in a race.

Within no more than two minutes Adrie came into the kitchen. "Oh, you frightened me," she said. "I peeked into the bedroom and you were not there."

"I couldn't sleep and I was hungry." I bit into the cookie so that my mouth would be full and Adrie wouldn't notice how my voice trembled. "How come you're back?"

"I forgot some important papers, and since I wasn't halfway there, I decided to come home and pick them up."

"So are you staying?" *Please don't stay, please don't stay,* I prayed. I took another bite of a cookie and realized how awful it tasted. It didn't matter; I swallowed hard and tried to look natural.

"I don't know. Maybe I'll have a cup of coffee and then head out again."

"I'll put the coffee on," I offered, getting up. I needed to spit out the cookie without her noticing.

At that moment Frieda came into the kitchen dressed in a chenille bathrobe. Watcher was at her feet, and he wiggled over to me, his tail wagging.

Adrie and Frieda spoke to each other, and I hoped Frieda wasn't coaxing her to stay home since it was so late. I swallowed the terrible cookie and tried not to show my distaste. Frieda filled the percolator and turned on the stove.

"I love driving in the night," I said. "I mean . . . um . . . the streets are not as busy, and there's a nice quiet world around me."

"Hmmm," Adrie said. "We'll see."

Frieda turned to look at me and noticed the second cookie on the table. She exclaimed something in German and grabbed the cookie.

"Frieda wants to know if you have eaten these cookies," Adrie said.

"Um . . . just one. I didn't care for it."

Frieda and Adrie spoke together and then began laughing. *What was so funny?* I wondered, wishing Adrie would just get up and leave. I couldn't bear it if she stayed overnight. She'd be sure to find that ladder standing in the library—not to mention the missing books in the closet.

"What's so funny?" I demanded, feeling sick with worry.

Frieda pointed to the cookie jar—still laughing.

Adrie turned to me. "Did you notice that cookie jar is a dog? That happens to be Watcher's cookie jar. Frieda made special dog cookies for Watcher, and you ate one."

I must have looked sick, because Adrie thrust a napkin into my hand.

"Oh, that is so funny." Adrie stretched her arms over her head. "I'm wide awake now, so I do think I'll head out." She spoke again in German, and Frieda, still laughing, turned off the stove.

"Let me help you out to the car," I offered.

"Oh, no. Just go back to bed."

I followed her out to the front door where she had her other briefcase waiting. The library door was closed, as I had left it. *Please don't go into the library. Please don't go into the library,* I prayed.

I didn't want to look anxious, so I breathed a pretend yawn and opened the front door for her. "Well, good night, Adrie. Have a safe trip." I stayed calm, smiled, and resisted a strong urge to push her out the door.

"Dog cookies! I'll probably laugh all the way to

Munich," she said as she headed out to the car. "Good night, Wendy."

"Good night!" I shut the door and heaved a deep breath.

22
The Dentist

The next morning, while Frieda was hanging clothes in the yard, and before I stashed away the books on the top shelf, I set aside one clear snapshot of the good-looking man who seemed to have been in love with Adrie. I wrapped it in an envelope and hid it between the pages of a book on the bookshelves. It would be hard to remember the name—*Die Leiden des jungen Werther* by Goethe—I'd have to go by the color—a deep green leather cover. After I tucked it in among the other books on a middle shelf, and put away the top-shelf books, I quietly set the ladder back in the closet.

Once I could relax, I went out to the terrace to look over my study book of the German language. I brought a dish of nuts to nibble on while I browsed through the vocabulary.

I will never get this language by myself, I decided.

Especially the pronunciation. In any case, with Johanna and Frieda to help me, I was finally getting the gist of what was being said—at least some of it.

I bit into a nut and *crack!* I spit into my napkin and looked through the brown pieces of the nut that I had chewed. To my horror, I discovered a large piece of white enamel. "My tooth!" I yelled. "Frieda!" I ran into the yard. "My tooth!"

I showed her what I had spewed into the napkin, then opened my mouth and pointed to my teeth. What was the German word for tooth? "*Zahn. Zahn.*"

Frieda understood. She pulled me to the sink in the laundry room and handed me a glass of water. "*Spülen.*"

I knew what she wanted. I rinsed my mouth and spit into the sink. I ran my tongue over my teeth when—ouch—a sharp edge on one of my back teeth nicked my tongue.

Frieda brought me out into the sunlight and peered into my mouth. She nodded and spoke sympathetically in German.

"What shall we do?" I asked.

As if she knew what I had said, Frieda went to the telephone and dialed. While she waited for an answer, she smiled at me and whispered, "*Mutter*—Adrie."

After speaking with Adrie and making two more phone calls, Frieda hustled me outside, where we waited for a taxi. Then off we went into town—to the dentist.

I hated going to the dentist. I tried faithfully to keep my teeth healthy so I wouldn't have to go—except to have them cleaned, of course. Cleaning didn't hurt too much.

Will he pull my tooth? Will he fill it? Will it hurt? Oh, I will never eat nuts again, I vowed.

As soon as I entered the dentist's office, I was marched into the big chair that I dreaded so much. The assistant, a tall blond woman, placed a bib around my neck without a word. She then arranged sharp-looking frightening instruments onto a tray, along with a paper cup of water. I could have used a smile or encouragement—but I never got either from her.

"Frieda!" I called loudly, realizing Frieda was not in the room with me. *"Kommen Sie her!"*

Frieda peeked in through the door and put her finger to her lips. "Shh."

The dentist, dressed in white, came into the room. "Ah, Wendy," he said. "I'm Dr. Kempka."

"You speak English?"

"Yes. I went to college in the States. Your mother called and said you chipped a tooth."

"Yes, I chipped a back tooth. Please, don't remove it. I've never even had a cavity."

"I'll need to see it before we decide anything," Dr. Kempka said. He came closer, turned on the light over my head, and then picked up a small mirror. "Open your mouth."

I lay stiffly in the chair while the doctor prodded and poked. He stuffed objects that felt like hard blocks of canvas into my mouth, put a lead apron over me, and then took X-rays of my teeth. I had never had X-rays before, and

I felt I would either choke on or throw up the clumps in my mouth.

Finally Dr. Kempka turned out the light and stepped back. “I can easily fix that tooth with a filling. The nerve is okay, but a large chip broke off. I’ll repair it right now, and then you can go home.” He patted my shoulder. “I’m going to give you Novocain. You won’t feel a thing while I repair that tooth.” He was holding something behind his back. “Close your eyes, take a deep breath, and relax.” He pushed something cold and metallic into my mouth and I felt a deep stab.

“Ow!” I yelped. “That hurt.”

“We’ll look at your X-rays while we wait for that Novocain to numb your tooth,” Dr. Kempka said, ignoring me. The assistant handed him negatives, which he looked at over lighted glass. “Hmm, you have an anomaly, Wendy. Did your regular dentist tell you that?”

“What’s an anomaly?”

“Well, my child, you have a tooth that is missing. It’s a genetic deformity.”

“What do you mean a deformity?”

Dr. Kempka grinned. “No one, not even you, would know you have this problem just by looking at you. Not yet, that is. Perhaps you’ve noticed that your tooth . . . Here . . . this lateral incisor . . .” He tapped on his own tooth. “This one that’s next to the center front tooth—on the right side—this is what you call a baby tooth in America. Here we call it *ein Milchzahn*—a milk tooth. In any case, it is a first tooth. You never lost it. Perhaps you've noticed it's smaller than your other teeth."

I thought for a moment. "Why, that's right. I don't remember ever losing that tooth."

"There's no adult tooth under it to push it out. The one that should be underneath is absent—congenitally absent—meaning you never had it. For now we will leave that milk tooth right where it is, but eventually it may come out by itself. Or it will need to be pulled. Then you'll need to have some correction—braces—and a false tooth on a bridge will be inserted. You'll never know it is false."

"A false tooth? Me? No, never!"

"If you don't, you'll have a gaping hole where it should be, and then your front teeth will move to the right, and your front teeth will be crooked. That wouldn't be at all becoming for a nice-looking girl like you."

Deformity? False teeth? I wanted to weep.

"Don't worry. That baby tooth is holding the space. But once that tooth does come out or is pulled out, you'll get it fixed then." Dr. Kempka set the chair back and adjusted the light. "Now we will fix that molar. You won't feel a thing."

Once the doctor had finished, I went out to the waiting room where Frieda was reading a magazine. The assistant spoke to Frieda in German, explaining what the doctor had done.

We were about to leave when Dr. Kempka came out. "Remember to keep an eye on that lateral incisor, Wendy."

"How did this happen?" I asked. "Why didn't that second tooth grow?"

"We don't really know why, but we do know it's hereditary. You probably got it from your mother or your father or even your grandparents."

"Adrie has perfect teeth. And my father's smile was beautiful."

"Then your grandparents might carry that gene. Take a good look at family photos and ask around the kinfolk. Perhaps you will find someone with a missing tooth who never had it fixed. You can tell—if the teeth are slanted to one side, if the missing tooth is in the same place as yours, that is."

He spoke to Frieda in German and then said to me. "You were a good patient, Wendy. Your mother left a number in Munich for me to call. Good-bye for now."

As usual, Watcher was so happy to have me home, he followed me everywhere. I got down on my knees and hugged my dog. "You and I are not perfect, Watcher," I told him. "Your ear doesn't stand up straight, and I have a missing tooth." He whined and lapped my face as if he understood. I kissed his floppy ear. "I love you just the same," I whispered.

Later that afternoon, when the Novocain wore off, I went around the house gathering the framed photographs of my father. I laid the photos on the kitchen table and turned the overhead light on high. Then, taking a magnifying glass from the drawer, I held it over my father's handsome face. Sure enough, in one picture where he was actually smiling, his teeth were perfectly even.

I didn't see anything that resembled a missing tooth or an off-center smile. So the dentist must have been wrong. I did not get that gene from my mother or my father. Hm. Of course, my father might have had a false tooth that didn't look like a false tooth. I would ask Adrie when she came home.

Then, with a start, I recalled the hidden photo of Adrie and that stranger. I grabbed the magnifying glass and darted into the library. I found the picture in the book where I had hidden it and brought it to the reading desk. I turned on the light and held the picture under the glass.

He sure was handsome, whoever he was, I thought as I held the glass to the face of the young man looking out at the sea from the yacht. Waves splashed against the bow, and the wind tousled his blond hair. I moved the magnifying glass away a bit to see his face even more clearly.

He had a nice smile and seemed to be having fun and laughing. No wonder my father wasn't smiling in many pictures if he knew Adrie was in love with this other man.

I looked again through the glass, studying the man's face and wide smile. I held the glass at another angle and concentrated on his teeth. Suddenly I felt my heart make an extra beat. His teeth were clearly visible in this photograph. I suddenly realized his teeth were not totally centered. They tilted to the right.

I checked more closely. The two front teeth were there, and on the left side was another tooth, which the dentist called the lateral incisor. Next to it I could see his eyetooth, but on the right side, he had no lateral incisor—only the eyetooth. The lateral incisor was missing! Mine wasn't missing yet, but if that baby tooth came out, I would have the same smile.

I grabbed the other photograph and paid attention to his teeth again. Yes, his teeth were exactly like mine would be once my baby tooth came out. I sat back in the chair while answers fell bit by bit into place, like a jigsaw puzzle.

The man in these pictures was my father!

23
My Heritage

I plopped down on my bed, suddenly tired, sad, and lonely.

Why did Adrie lie about my father? It seemed as if my whole life had been lies. Should I demand she tell me everything, based upon what I found out in the albums? Adrie would be furious that I had searched those off-limits books. Still, I had a right to know who my father was, didn't I?

I decided to do nothing at all. I would not say a word. I would just go on keeping my own secrets—as Adrie had all these years.

I thought about Herr Strohkirch, who seemed to know everything about me. What had he said about my father? I closed my eyes and tried to recall his words . . . *a kind, gentle man. He was not the man you think he was.* That certainly turned out to be the truth!

Herr Strohkirch had said he would be there when I was ready to listen. Well, I am ready, and the only place I knew to reach him is in the park. *Therefore, I must go to the park today and hope that he or Barret will be there,* I decided.

After dressing I went to the kitchen where Frieda had made oatmeal. Watcher came out from his bed under the table to greet me, his tail wagging.

"We're going for a walk," I told him, "right after breakfast." I filled his dish with a can of horse meat, which he gobbled up eagerly. Then he went to the door and looked back at me, as if to ask, *Shall we go?*

I let him out into the fenced-in yard. Then I ate my breakfast while Frieda sat opposite me, sipping on coffee and reading the morning newspaper. She was shaking her head at the headlines. I had no idea what was going on with the war, but from Frieda's expression, the news was not good. Of course, that would depend on whose side you were on. I wasn't on any side. I was neutral, like Johanna.

Frieda spoke to me in little German phrases, and I was able to answer her. I could tell she was proud that I had learned so many words, as well as the expressions she had taught me. Now I was finding that words came without my even trying. Still, I could not come up with the total language yet; it was hard to understand Frieda, or anyone, when they spoke German rapidly.

After breakfast I called *"Ich gehe!"* to Frieda to let her know Watcher and I were taking a walk, and then we headed out to the park. I tucked the photograph of the man I believed to be my father deep into the pocket of my sweater. Would Barret and his grandfather be there?

When I entered the park, I noticed how empty and still it was. The birds were silent. As Watcher and I walked through each vacant pathway, our footsteps clicked noisily on the pavement. There was no one there but us.

If only I had made a definite arrangement to meet them! However, at the time, I couldn't really be certain of what Herr Strohkirch was trying to tell me.

Disappointed, I sat on the bench by the fountain, still hoping that Herr Strohkirch and Barret would show up. Since I had not slept the night before, the warm sun made me drowsy. Watcher had already stretched out, his head on his paws, his eyes closed.

Then . . . there they were! Barret leaned on his grandfather's arm as they walked slowly into the park. In his other hand, instead of holding Heidi's leash, Barret carried a white cane.

I jumped up as they came through the gate. "Thank goodness, you're here. I have so much to tell you."

Barret did not have his dark glasses on, and I noticed how he looked toward my voice. His eyes were a deep blue. "Wendy?"

"Yes, it's me, Wendy," I said. "How did you know I'd be here?"

"We didn't know, but we have walked here every day wondering if we would ever see you again," Herr Strohkirch said as he led Barret to my bench. Barret felt for the seat with his hand, and then we sat together.

"Where's Heidi?" I asked.

Barret's face saddened. "The SS took Heidi away from me and gave her to a soldier who lost his sight in combat. The SS officer who took Heidi said, 'A brave soldier has given his sight for the Reich. The least you can do is give him your dog.' He was right, of course."

"Oh, Barret, I'm so sorry. What will you do?" I reached for his hand.

"I don't know. I feel useless without her. She was my best friend."

"Watcher and I are your friends," I said, feeling his sadness. I snapped my fingers, and Watcher sat up and put his chin on Barret's lap. "See? Watcher is reminding you he is still your friend."

Barret patted my dog's head and ears. "Watcher, you still have that floppy ear," he said, managing a grin.

Herr Strohkirch sat down with us. "Time is becoming more and more urgent, Wendy. I am old and do not have much time left in this world. The way things are, I will not be sorry to leave. I have helped Jews and others leave this country, so who knows when my own questionable acts will be found out by the police. Now I must fulfill my promise to your father. But first I am sure you have questions."

"Yes, I do have many questions."

"I must again stress that Adrie must never know about our meeting or that I have divulged the information I'm about to give you."

"I don't understand why it's such a secret or why she hasn't told me herself."

"One of her missions in life is to protect you."

"Why do I need protection?"

Herr Strohkirch looked uncomfortable. "Because of who you are."

I pulled the photograph from my pocket with my free hand and handed it to Herr Strohkirch. "Who is this man?"

He took a pair of glasses from his jacket pocket and put them on. He smiled as he examined the photograph and then looked up at me. "This is David Dressner, your father."

I sat between Barret and his grandfather. I stared at the photograph of my father while I listened at last to the story of my heritage.

"Your mother was very young when she met David. She was extremely bright and had learned several languages at the University of Munich. At that time she met a brilliant young geology professor and they fell in love." Herr Strohkirch cleared his throat and then added, "But then, as now, it was a complicated and dangerous thing for a young German woman to fall in love—with a Jewish man."

"Jewish?" I pointed to the photo. "Was this man . . . my father . . . a Jew?"

Herr Strohkirch nodded. "*Ja.* Your father, David Dressner, was indeed a Jew."

My father was a Jew and that made me Jewish, too. Jews were hated in Germany. Johanna had whispered to me that terrible things were happening to the Jews.

I was a Jewish girl living in Nazi Germany. Fear crept over me like the pitiless spider weaving its evil web.

24
The Whole Truth

For fifteen years, I was Wendy Taylor, then I was Wendy Dekker, and now I discover I am really Wendy Dressner and the daughter of a Jew. I was beginning to understand why Adrie did not want me to know. It was dangerous to be Jewish here in Germany.

Barret's grandfather continued. "At first it didn't matter to Adrie that David was Jewish, but it did matter to Adrie's family. Throughout history, people in many nations have persecuted Jews. Whenever a predicament arose, be it a crime or a plague, an official government crisis, or some small issue, it was usually Jews who were accused. That hatred was handed down from generation to generation. Then along came Adrie and David—and none of it mattered. They were in love. Still, they were aware of the controversies this would cause for their families so they kept their relationship and marriage a secret."

Barret's grandfather paused to take out his pipe and stuff it with tobacco. Then, after lighting it, he continued with the story—my story.

"So despite everything, they did get married?" I asked.

"Let me see." He counted on his fingers. "About seven years before you were born—back in 1920, Hitler announced to the Nazi party that no Jews should be considered citizens. David predicted what would soon happen to Jews and he was right, because in 1935, the Nuremberg Laws were passed, and Jews lost their rights as German citizens. Shortly after that, marriage between Jews and non-Jews was forbidden. Before long, Jews were removed from all the universities."

"And it got worse, didn't it, Opa?" Barret added. "Shops and restaurants stopped serving Jews. There were signs in restaurants and hotels: JEWS NOT ADMITTED. In some places they couldn't use public transportation or parks."

"Like our negros in the South," I admitted. "I've never been in the South, but I've been told they still separate blacks from whites in public parks and restaurants and buses." None of this had meant much to me, as I had been growing up in northern New York. Now that I discovered I was Jewish, I began to realize how it must feel to be singled out and hated.

"I don't feel any different than I ever did, and I don't mind being Jewish. But I'm living here and now I am scared." Tears suddenly brimmed in my eyes, and I struggled to keep them from slipping down my cheeks. "This must be the reason Adrie stressed to me over and over that I am pure German and pure Aryan. She's afraid someone might find out I'm Jewish."

"Adrie would be in deep trouble, too, especially considering her position in the *Abwehr*, which is similar to the Office of Strategic Services in your country." Herr Strohkirch shook his head. "She has many reasons to keep this secret, and she'll be furious if she finds out I've revealed all this to you."

"There's one thing I don't understand," I said. "Why is Adrie so loyal to Hitler? She adores her Führer. She believes in the Socialist Party Master Race and a thousand-year order ruled by Germans."

Herr Strohkirch took a puff of his pipe and looked thoughtful. "You need to realize how destitute Germany was after the Great War. When the Treaty of Versailles was signed, Germany was blamed for everything. Germans had to pay for all the damages and costs of the war. There were other reparations too. We were allowed only a small army; we could not fly planes. The country was poor and hated. No one had money. There were no jobs.

"Then along came Adolf Hitler and his socialist party. He made promises; he reminded the German people they were 'the master race.' He built up the country with work and jobs—and gave everyone hope. People listened to his speeches and gained confidence again. They came to believe and have faith in Hitler, as if he were a prophet from God who had come to save the nation. Brilliant scientists and educators look to him, believe in him, and are willing to do anything he asks."

"And that's what happened to Adrie?"

"She is one of the strongest believers of all. She even turned away from David—your father—when he was imprisoned."

Barret added, "I've heard people who watch the Führer parade by collect the dirt he walked on to keep as a shrine in their houses."

Something Johanna said came back to me. *Heil Hitler means you worship Hitler as your savior.* No wonder Johanna refused to say *Heil Hitler*. He was the man who started this war of killing and hatred. Yet despite that, the people adored him.

"You must never tell anyone about our talk today," Herr Strohkirch reminded me. "Anything overheard can mean your imprisonment and for me . . . possibly death."

"Then why search for me to tell me all this?" I felt a trace of anger. "I was perfectly okay with who I was. Now I'm afraid."

"I'm informing you of this because of the promise I made to your father before he died in prison. He wanted you to know your birthright, and he hoped Adrie would never bring you to Germany. If she did, however, he gave me instructions to get you out of the country to safety—if it ever became necessary."

Out of the country? Did that mean I could go home and be Wendy Taylor again? An American girl? "Can I leave whenever I want?"

"Oh, my dear, of course not. No one can just up and leave. Besides, Adrie would never let you go."

"So I must stay here forever?"

"Not necessarily, but to escape would take careful planning. The borders are closely guarded, and it would be dangerous. However, now that you know all the parts of the puzzle, it is an option that you can hold in your heart until you decide. Your father wanted you to have that choice. If you do decide to leave at some point, I will help you—just as I promised David.

"For now the best thing for you is to go on being Adrie's perfect Aryan daughter—a true German girl, just as Adrie wants for you," Herr Strohkirch advised. "Or at least pretend to be."

"I sometimes wish I could go back to New York," I said wistfully. "I feel guilty that I left my mom and daddy over there without a word, after all they did for me. I miss them."

"Never speak of your New York family or friends, and never say that things were better in the States. Especially don't say that you resent certain aspects of the Third Reich," Barret warned me. "Isn't that true, Opa?"

"*Ja*," his grandfather agreed. "People betray one another here. It is dangerous to speak out."

I thought again of Johanna, who was German—who had done nothing wrong except worship God and read the Bible. Yet she was not free, and the rest of her family was in prison because they would not pretend or deny who they were. Now I felt as if I were in a prison, because I had to hide my thoughts and words . . . and who I really was. There was no freedom here in Germany for anyone who did not agree with Herr Hitler, I realized. Even for Germans.

I wondered again about my real father. "Tell me more about David Dressner—my father."

Herr Strohkirch nodded. "Oh, he was very concerned about your future even before you were born. He didn't want you to live as a *Mischling* here in Germany for the rest of your life."

"What is a *Mischling*?"

"A half-Jew—it means 'half-breed' or . . ." Barret hesitated.

"Mongrel!" Herr Strohkirch spit out the English word. "*Ach!* How disgusting—to give that name to any human being." He looked away for a moment, waved his hand as if casting off a bit of dirt, and then continued with my parents' story. "David and Adrie both agreed that you should have every opportunity of a happy, safe life. There was only one way out of the situation."

I instantly knew the solution. "That's when Adrie married Karl Dekker and pretended he was my father?"

"Correct!" Strohkirch smiled. "Karl Dekker was a wounded Great War hero and had always been in love with Adrie. Adrie agreed to marry him right away. As an official in the government, I was able to secretly destroy all records of Adrie and David's marriage."

"So Karl believed I was his daughter?"

"*Ja.* Karl was a good man. Later Adrie went to New York, where you were born, and took on your aunt and uncle's surname, Taylor. Adrie and Karl together decided it would be safer for you to stay in the United States for a period of time because the government here was unpredictable at that point."

Herr Strohkirch relit the tobacco in his pipe. "Eventually poor Karl died from his war injuries. He received the Iron Cross for valor. As far as the world is concerned, you are Karl's daughter. It's never been necessary for anyone to know differently."

"Did my real father, David, ever meet me?"

"*Nein*—no. I received photographs from New York that I brought to David. He called you his *Liebling*—his darling child."

I looked again at the picture of my father, David Dressner, and at his pleasant smile. "Was it David who gave my mother the ruby ring?"

"*Ja.* His family owned a string of fine-jewelry stores. After his expulsion from the university as a geologist, he worked in the Netherlands, where he traded worldwide. He collected some of the most valuable gems in the world—like that ruby. David designed the ring in pure twenty-four karat gold. It's worth a fortune."

"Adrie told me about the value of the pigeon-blood ruby when she gave me the ring and told me I was her daughter."

Barret, who had been listening intently, spoke up. "That tells you how much you mean to Adrie."

"Be careful with that ring." Herr Strohkirch's expression darkened. "It could be stolen by the government. Reichsmarschall Göring takes wealth and treasures belonging to the Jews for his own personal collection. He has also helped himself to many of the world's most precious art collections."

"*Ja.* Just as they took Heidi from me," Barret murmured in a low voice. "They said that the soldier who lost his sight was far more . . . er . . . *wertvoll* . . . valuable than a blind boy like me."

"How dare they say such a cruel thing?" I blurted out. "You are valuable and . . . bright and kind." To my own surprise—as well as Barret's—I threw my arms around him and hugged him.

25
Grandfather

I hoped Barret could tell how embarrassed I was for my impulsive show of affection. "I'm sorry, Barret. Please forgive me." I could feel my own face burning, and I had to look away.

However, I was relieved and happy when Barret changed the subject. "I live within walking distance. I would enjoy meeting you again here or somewhere. We can walk and visit, and I'd be happy to help you train your dog."

"Does Adrie know you live nearby, Herr Strohkirch?" I asked Barret's grandfather. "She'll be away for another week or so, but after that, she might suspect I am meeting someone if I come down here too often."

"I've moved several times since Adrie and David knew me. She has no idea that I'm living nearby. Barret has lived with me since his father died."

I turned to Barret. "I'm sorry, Barret. I didn't realize you had lost your father."

"*Danke*, Wendy," he replied.

"And your mother? Is she living?"

"Barret's mother, Adrienne, was my beautiful daughter," Herr Strohkirch said. "My only child."

"My mother died when I was born," Barret explained. "I was very small, premature, and in fact, that is the reason I am blind. My grandfather has been good to me, and I know it is hard for my Opa to have a blind grandson to"—Barret struggled for the right words in English—"to care for."

"*Ach*, you are my joy. You know that, Barret." His grandfather grasped Barret's shoulder, and for a moment I saw tears well up in Herr Strohkirch's eyes.

"You call your grandfather 'Opa'?" I asked, trying to brighten the conversation.

"*Ja*, that's like 'granddad' in your country," Barret said.

Herr Strohkirch smiled. "You may call me Opa too, Wendy. Herr Strohkirch is . . . what you would say in America . . . is a mouthful. I will be your grandfather, and we three will be a family."

"*Ja* and it would be better not to use the name Strohkirch at all," Barret added. "Opa has an important position in the Third Reich. We do not want him to get in trouble for the help he gives so many people."

"Shall we meet here on Tuesday and Thursday afternoons, since I work on Mondays, Wednesdays, and Fridays?" Then I wondered how he could manage his way to the park without a dog. "Will Opa come with you?"

"Sometimes. He often works at the Chancellery. Do not worry about me walking by myself, Wendy. I can see light and the shadows of people and cars," he assured me. "It's not as if I'm in total darkness. I will use my white cane. I know my way here very well—by heart. In fact, I could walk here . . . how you say it . . . blindfolded." He laughed. "About ten o'clock on Tuesday morning?"

"That sounds right. By the way, how do you tell time—other than asking someone?" I asked curiously.

Barret put his arm out to show me the watch on his wrist. He popped the glass open with a click and then touched the hands inside. "Right now it's ten past eleven. Right? Notice how the numbers are raised little bumps. They're in Braille."

I moved closer to see. "Oh, so you read Braille?"

"Oh, *ja,* since I was very young."

"Once he caught on, there was no stopping him," Opa said with a proud smile. "He reads everything he can find that's in Braille."

I was beginning to understand how well Barret could get along by himself.

Opa stood, waiting to leave. "Shall we go now, Barret?"

"*Ja,* I suppose we should." As Barret reached for his grandfather's arm, Watcher got up from his place at my feet and lapped Barret's hand. "We will train you to be the best dog in Berlin, Watcher," Barret told him.

I batted Barret's arm. "He already is the best dog in Berlin!"

Opa paused on his way to the sidewalk. "Before we go, I must remind you again that our conversations here must be kept private. Lives depend upon that, Wendy, my dear." Opa's eyes were serious.

"I understand, Opa." I knew very well what Adrie might do if she knew what Opa had revealed to me. Adrie could be dangerous. Opa, especially, would be in danger.

"If you are not here, I will understand that you cannot come," Barret said. "We will find a way to keep in touch—if you need me."

I had a sudden rush of relief mixed with joy. I had a friend—and a grandfather.

26
Reasons to Be Happy

Watcher and I walked home slowly. I had so much to straighten out in my head. I understood now who my true father was and why Adrie had kept him a secret. What scared me the most was the hush-hush talk about the death camps. When Johanna and I sat outside and ate lunch together one day, she whispered to me terrible things about the death camps, where she said Jews—even children—were killed by the thousands. Surely, the German people would never allow death camps or such awful things to happen, would they?

In any case, what did it have to do with me? I would never tell anyone I was Jewish.

By now we had walked around the block and approached the driveway of my house. I stopped and looked at the tall beautiful stone mansion. My bedroom here was bigger than the whole first floor of my old house in New York. I had everything I needed or wanted. I loved the house and Frieda and the wonderful meals she made. I loved having a dog, even during the war, when many people did not have enough to eat but my dog was well fed. Should I feel guilty? No. It wasn't my fault that there was a war or that people were starving and imprisoned. Besides, what could I do about it?

I jingled the bracelet on my arm, the one with the three gold monkeys. *See no evil. Hear no evil. Speak no evil.*

From now on I wouldn't be alarmed at what I heard or saw. I had every reason to be happy. I would stay right here and be the daughter Adrie wanted.

With that decision, I felt better. I bent down to pet Watcher, who looked up at me sweetly and lapped my face.

"Let's go home, Watcher," I said.

In the fenced-in yard, I took off Watcher's leash, found a stout twig, and threw the stick across the grass. My dog leaped, snatched it in midair, and brought it back to me. I repeated the game for several minutes. Then, without thinking, I tossed the stick too high and watched as it hurtled over the hedge between our property and the house next door. Watcher ran after the twig, his eyes on it as it spun through the air. Then he came to a stop at the thick bushes, puzzled, as if wondering where his toy had gone. He looked back at me questioningly.

"I'm sorry, Watcher," I called. "Let's go inside now."

However, Watcher still sniffed the ground and lawn beneath the hedgerow. Suddenly he vanished into the greenery. I ran to where Watcher had disappeared, got down on my knees, and peered under the thick hedge. Watcher was tunneling his way under the branches and roots, scratching and pawing through to the opposite side.

"Come back, Watcher!" I called. *"Komm züruk!"* I stood up and brushed the dirt from my hands. Now I'd have to go out to the street and around to the next house to get him.

Just then I heard more scratching. I peered under the hedge again. Watcher was on his way back. He scrunched down as flat as he could make himself, while his front and back legs pushed him frantically through the shallow tunnel he had created. All the while he gripped his stick in his mouth. I couldn't help laughing as he made his way through the tangles of leaves and dirt. Once free of his leafy tunnel, he stood up and shook off the twigs and soil. Then, with his tail wagging wildly, he dropped the stick at my feet.

"Oh, thank you, Watcher. *Guter Hund!*" I laughed and hugged him. *"Guter Hund."*

Frieda called from the door. "Wendy. *Abendessen!*"

I clapped my hands at Watcher, who sat at my feet, tail still wagging. "Dinner is ready, Watcher. Let's go."

After washing my hands at the stone sink, I plunked myself at the table. *"Oh,* Frieda, *Ich bin am Verhungern!"* I spread a slice of homemade bread with butter and stuffed it into my mouth.

I realized I had said, "I'm starving," in German. How did I know those words without even thinking? Typically, I had to think hard to put the German words together, or struggle to find the right word. It was just as Adrie had said—that suddenly, without realizing it, I was speaking German words and sentences. Turning to Frieda I said, "Frieda, *Ich spreche Deutsch!* I speak German!"

Frieda poured some tea for both of us then held up her cup as if making a toast. *"Prost,* Wendy*!"*

"Prost!" I responded happily. "Cheers!"

Adrie stayed in Munich for the next several weeks, so I was able to alternate my weekdays between Lebensborn and meeting Barret. He and I took walks around the park or down the street to the hospital, where we also found pleasant walkways to sit and talk. He had a personal name for me in both German and English. "Wendy Vendy!" I loved hearing him tease me and call me Wendy Vendy.

Barret and I worked with Watcher, teaching him to pause at street corners or at the edge of sidewalks. When walking with me, Watcher veered me away protectively from other people who passed by. We rewarded Watcher with Frieda's dog cookies.

We talked about our lives growing up. I told him about Mom and Daddy in New York, my school and my friends. I related what had happened in Maine with the malicious girls there, and about my friend Jill and her famous father, the singer Drew Winters.

Barret told me about his years in England and how he came back to Germany . . . to attend his father's funeral.

Several times Barret confided in me his feelings and

fears about the Third Reich. That was when I told him my decision to "see no evil, speak no evil, and hear no evil" like the three wise monkeys on my bracelet. "I want to be happy. I am going to block out all the horrible things I hear."

He listened, then reached for my hand. "Wendy Vendy, be happy, but don't hide from the truth."

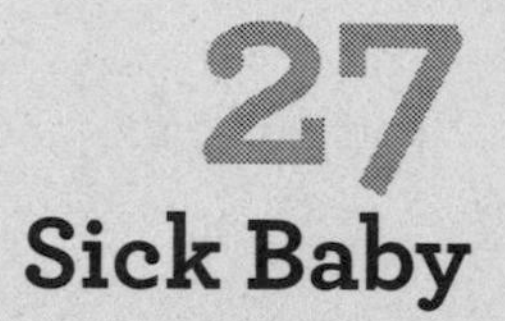

Sick Baby

One morning I arrived at Lebensborn as a few young children were eating breakfast at their little tables. Hunfrid, who was with them, didn't seem to be eating.

I went to Hunfrid, took his spoon, dipped it into the oatmeal, and held the spoon to his lips.

"*Nein.*" He turned his head away.

"Aren't you hungry?" I asked. I noticed his flushed face and runny nose, then put my hand to his forehead. "You're burning up with fever, poor baby!" I whispered. I looked around, hoping to see Frau Messner or Johanna. There was no one to help, so I gathered him into my arms and headed for the nursery.

After setting Hunfrid into a crib, I filled a small basin with water from a nearby tub. I pulled Hunfrid's shirt up, dipped the cloth in the cool water, and was about to wipe his hot little back and chest when he began to shudder violently. His head fell back, his eyes rolled, and his body arched. At that moment Hunfrid threw up, the vomit spewing out all over the crib and me. "He's convulsing!" I yelled in English, not knowing the word for "convulsing" in German.

A nurse came, grabbed the wet face cloth from me, and wiped Hunfrid's mouth and his stiff, trembling body. Then, snatching him from the crib, she raced to the set tub, and shoved him into the water. Slowly, the little boy's tremors subsided. The nurse splashed water and soap over him, wrapped a towel around him, and carried him back to another, clean crib.

I asked, "What's wrong?" in German. She answered me but spoke so fast, I could not follow all her words. I was ready to cry myself, when Johanna appeared. She looked me up and down, and I realized how I must look and smell with my clothes covered with vomit.

"Johanna, little Hunfrid is so sick. He had convulsions."

Johanna's shoulders sank and she shook her head. "Oh, no! He must not get sick," she responded in English.

"For goodness' sake, it's not his fault," I said. "Is there a doctor here?"

The nurse standing nearby understood. *"Ja. Doktor,"* she said, leaving the room.

Johanna pointed to a nearby lavatory and said, "Go clean up, and I'll change Hunfrid."

In the bathroom I took off my clothes, washed up, and a found a pile of clean housedress uniforms on a shelf. I put one on, stuffed my own clothing into a bag, and went back to Hunfrid's crib. A woman doctor had arrived and was listening to his heart and lungs. I recognized her. It was Dr. Ernst—Gertrude Ernst's mother. She didn't seem to recognize me.

"Is he all right?" I asked in German.

"He is not well, this boy." She pointed to his thin body and shook her head. "He is German, right?"

"He is . . . ," I began.

Johanna quickly cut me off. "There are many cold germs going around," she said. "Several children have come down with this. I'm sure he will be fine." Johanna held Hunfrid up while Dr. Ernst poured a tablespoon of liquid into his mouth. He coughed and sputtered, then looked up at me helplessly. I felt helpless too.

"We must give him this every four hours," Johanna said after Dr. Ernst left. She set the medicine on a nearby table.

"Why did you say he must not get sick, Johanna?"

Johanna whispered. "Don't you understand, Wendy? He's not German. We have to keep him well and healthy. If he's sickly and doesn't fit in as a German child . . ." Her voice trailed off, but I could hear every word. "They won't waste more time or money on a little Polish boy."

I never left Hunfrid's bedside all day. Although he slept most of the time, once or twice he opened his eyes and looked for me. When he saw I was there, he went quietly back to sleep.

I wondered about his mother and how she must be missing him—and then I remembered hearing his mother was dead. "Do you know what happened to Hunfrid's mother?" I asked Johanna when she came by to see how I was doing.

Johanna shook her head. "Oh, Wendy, she was shot and killed when she tried to grab him away from the SS officer who took him. Hunfrid is a perfect Aryan. Blond hair, blue eyes. He looks German."

"I thought the war was being fought for . . . land, power, or other things. But kidnapping a baby because he is blue-eyed and blond, and then killing his mother? That's too terrible to bear, and I am trying not to believe or even listen to such horrible stories."

Johanna put her arm around me. "It is horrible, Wendy. Yet, it is true."

I recalled Barret's words to me: *Don't hide from the truth, Wendy.*

28
The Silent Ones

"Things may work out well for Hunfrid," Johanna said with a bright smile that I knew was meant to cheer me up. "Many Germans adopt or at least care for Lebensborn babies. In fact, an SS officer and his wife have come in several times to see Hunfrid. I wouldn't be at all surprised if they decide to take him home."

"Were they kind? Did he like them?"

"They thought he was sweet and intelligent. They played with him, and he was laughing and being merry. He seems happy when they come to visit him."

"What if no one takes him? What will happen to him? How long will Lebensborn take care of him?"

"If he stays well, maybe . . ." Johanna turned away. "I do not know. I hear . . . terrible things." She stopped as if considering whether to tell me. Then she whispered, "Remember, there are death camps where thousands and thousands of people—including mothers and babies—are murdered every day."

"If this is all true, why don't the German people do something? It's as if there's a big secret that everyone knows but no one talks about."

Johanna nodded. "Those who know are afraid for their own lives, so they close their eyes and ears to the horrors going on here. However, God knows and sees everything. He will see that this wickedness ends."

I was suddenly angry with God—wherever he was. "God is silent too!"

"He's not silent. He is using people who risk their lives to get the truth of what is going on here out the world—as well as bringing God's message of hope for the future. Trust me, Wendy. God is not silent."

"How can you go on, being helpful and upbeat, even though you and your family are imprisoned?"

"I believe that God is watching and he will end the atrocities in his own time." She gave me a hug and went back to work. Somehow she always had a way of making me feel better.

Before I left Lebensborn late that afternoon, I washed Hunfrid's hot little body with cool water, dressed him in clean pajamas, and rocked him until he fell asleep.

I was getting up to leave when I noticed two new girls had arrived and were putting their jackets into the closet. When they turned around, I recognized them from the tea party reception. It was Gertrude Ernst and her sidekick,

Rikka Himmelman. I turned away quickly, but they saw me.

"Isn't that Wendy Dekker?" Gertrude muttered in German to her friend. "I'm surprised that they trust an American to work here." She bitterly spit out the word *American*.

"*Ja*. Will we need to work with her?"

"Of course not. We are here to . . . Johanna . . . *Bibelforscher*."

I strained my ears but could not hear the rest of Gertrude's words. However, I did hear Johanna's name and the word *Bibelforscher*—the name for the Bible Students who were being imprisoned and killed. Gertrude and Rikka were here to make trouble for my friend Johanna!

The two girls probably didn't know I saw them or that I could speak German pretty well now. So, without a word, I quickly went into the nursery where Johanna was working.

"Hunfrid's asleep," she said gently, when she saw me. "He'll be fine now, Wendy. Don't worry."

"Johanna, do you know there are two girls who have come to work with you?" I asked in a hushed voice.

"No," she said with a slight frown. "Why? Who are they?"

"Trouble," I whispered. After telling her what I overheard, I cautioned her. "I think they are here to trap you."

Johanna nodded. "Oh, *ja*. This happened with Frau Messner when I first came. She eventually began to trust me and leave me alone. But she may try again if she is put under pressure. There are others who want to put me in prison and then force me to reveal who my friends are and where they may be meeting for our worship." She shook her head. "All my family and most of my dearest friends are in prison. I have no idea if or where the rest are able to meet. And I would never tell them even if I did know."

"Don't let those two girls trick you, Johanna."

"Thank you for warning me, Wendy. I will be careful."

On the way home I waited for the bus and noticed a girl standing nearby. The same girl who begged outside of Lebensborn. She was still looking for money to buy a uniform for the youth group. I did not have much money with me, so I turned away from her. I noticed a few other passengers did put a coin or two into her box. She did not get on the bus when it came. Instead she turned and walked away, stopping people on the sidewalk to ask for money.

I climbed on board, found a seat, and watched the people around me. Many were going to a late shift; others, who were probably going home, looked tired—some of them even sleeping in their seats. A few were reading a newspaper, and some laughed or spoke with one another. Most, though, were silent.

Did any of them know that thousands of innocent people were being murdered every day in death camps? Johanna said her *Bibelforscher* friends were risking their lives to get the truth out to the world. Perhaps many of the Germans refused to believe that Jews were being slaughtered, or they chose to ignore the stories. How could they live their lives knowing this terrible secret? Why didn't they cry out? Why did they stay silent?

Then I remembered that I had my own secret.

I was a Jew—a *Mischling*. If I valued my life, I had to live a lie and stay silent too.

29
The White Rose Students

Adrie was gone for three weeks. She was back and unpacking her suitcase when I arrived home one Friday. She pulled a garnet-red dress from her suitcase and tossed it to me. "This is perfect for you. Go try it on."

The dress was simple, with long sleeves, and trimmed with white lace at the collar and sleeves. I loved the material—soft and comfortable. The label said *Jugendliche*. Didn't that mean young, or teenage? Why did Adrie have this dress in her suitcase? Her clothes were usually very sophisticated—and very stylish but this was a dress for a younger person.

I ran to my room, quickly changed, and looked in the full-length mirror, turning slowly. It was beautiful.

"Schön!" Adrie agreed when she popped into my room.

"Did you buy it for me?" I asked.

"No. I wore it once. . . ." She paused as if determining

whether to tell me. Then she went on. "When I was in Munich, my assignment was to become a student at the university." She smiled but then looked serious. "It was difficult, because I couldn't get one soul to open up about the White Rose group—such as who was involved and who helped them."

"What are they doing that is so terrible?"

"They are writing and passing out antigovernment leaflets that are full of hatred for our Führer, the SS, and the Reich in general. The group is stirring up dissenters and is growing in numbers. They've got to be silenced."

She took a deep breath. "I was hoping one of them would give themselves away, but they are a very tight, dedicated group."

I twirled around in front of the mirror, trying not to appear too interested in the White Rose group. "So you became a student again. "

"Yes, I did, and in case you are wondering if I got away with it—they all accepted me completely. I even went to student parties." Her expression became grave. "Believe me, it wasn't fun, knowing that group would be found out sooner or later. God help those students when they're caught . . . and they will be caught."

She left the room, and I called out, "Thank you for the dress. But wherever will I wear it?"

"At Reichsmarschall Himmler's birthday party," she replied.

"What?"

"October seventh is his birthday, and I'm sure there

will be a party at Lebensborn. After all, he is the one who created the Lebensborn program."

That was next week! I wondered how Johanna would get by on that day with Gertrude and Rikka there.

After supper Adrie said, "I'm going to listen to the British newscast." She headed for the den and then paused. "Oh, by the way, pay close attention to this, Wendy." She emphasized each word. "If any citizen is caught listening to international broadcasts, they will be shot."

"Oh, come on. You're kidding me, aren't you?"

"No, it's true. The false news we get from the allied countries makes German people depressed and stirs up fear that we might lose the war, which could not be further from the truth." She gave me a warning look. "So I don't want you listening anymore."

"What about you? You're always listening to British broadcasts."

"I'm allowed to listen because of my position with the *Abwehr*." Adrie headed for the den. "Just remember, no sneaking into my den to hear British broadcasts anymore."

That made me angry, and I stomped after her into the den. "I never sneak in here. And I only listened when you were listening."

"There's more," Adrie went on. "American jazz and American music by that . . . what's his name . . . Glenn Miller—they're forbidden too."

"Glenn Miller? You mean 'In the Mood' and 'Chattanooga Choo Choo'?"

"Yes, all his music—and other American performers as well."

I never heard the U.S. Government tell us what music we could listen to. I opened my mouth in protest but changed my mind. There was no point in arguing with Adrie.

"Oh, Wendy. I'm just warning you . . . so no one will shoot you." Suddenly, as if trying to make things lighter, she grinned and held up her fingers like a gun. "Bang!" she said.

That is not funny, I thought as I marched out of the den.

30
Lady-Bird, Fly Away Home

The next morning at Lebensborn, Hunfrid ran to see me with a big grin on his face. I was relieved to see he had recovered so well. He was thin and pale, but his smile was bright and beautiful.

What a darling little boy. His life was so sad. Nothing bad should ever happen to him again!

During the afternoon the officer from the SS and his wife, the couple Johanna had spoken about, came to see Hunfrid. When they called his German name, his face lit up and he raced to meet them. For a while I was extremely jealous.

Johanna was talking with the couple, explaining how sick he had been. I could see concern on the woman's face, and she picked him up, cuddled him, and kissed his cheek.

Be glad someone loves him, and wants him, I scolded

myself. *He needs a home, even if it's not his own home.*

I recalled my aunt Nixie—my New York mom—who had been my mother all my life. I was a happy little girl, and I felt loved. Hunfrid would be happy too. I turned away and went into the nursery where the other children needed me.

Later when I looked for Hunfrid, I didn't see him anywhere. Johanna put her arm around me and whispered, "He has gone. He has a family again, Wendy, so feel happy for him."

I sat on the chair I had used to rock him to sleep, and cried for a little while.

Afterward I turned my thoughts to those deceitful girls, Rikka and Gertrude. They hadn't shown up yet, so I hoped they had lost interest in whatever they were scheming. I was certain it had to do with Johanna.

Meanwhile, Johanna took out her little accordion. The children squealed happily and sat at her feet while she sang nursery rhymes. They smiled and sang with her, their hands clapping to the music.

Then Johanna looked at me and said in English, "This song is for you, Wendy. Listen carefully to this verse." She began to sing:

Fly back again, back again, lady-bird dear!
Thy neighbors will merrily welcome thee here;
The children will dance and the skies will be bright;
You will find peace and love in the still of the night.
And there shall no perils attend thee!

The next day, when I met Barret, I told him about Johanna's riddle for me and asked him what he thought it meant.

"It is your riddle, Wendy Vendy. What do you think she is saying?"

"That somehow, I should leave Germany and go back to America."

31
Danger Ahead for Johanna

I wore my new red dress to Lebensborn on Wednesday. I was sad because I knew little Hunfrid was no longer there. I would miss his voice calling to Johanna and me: "Ven-dee— Yo Yo!" I hoped with all my heart that he was safe and happy.

As soon as I entered the building, I looked for Johanna. Were Gertrude Ernst and Rikka Himmelman there with their evil plans to cause trouble for her?

I went to the playroom, hoping Johanna was there—but she was not. Instead Gertrude Ernst stood by the window, her arms across her chest, a cold, arrogant look on her face. Did I dare ask about Johanna? I was afraid to know what they might have done.

Frau Messner was walking among the children as I approached her. "*Guten Morgen,* Frau Messner," I said in German.

"Oh, Wendy, what a pretty dress! You speak so well in German now. I can see you have a gift for languages like your mother does," Frau Messner said with a half-smile.

"Thanks to Johanna," I answered. "She's been my tutor and mentor. She's made learning German a pleasure." Even though Frau Messner was smiling, I could tell something was bothering her. "Where is Johanna?" I asked, looking around.

Frau Messner gathered herself together, and a stern look came over her face. "She is being punished."

"Why?"

"Because she will not give in and sign her paper, that's why."

"But that's been her stand all along. Why is she being punished today?"

"I've been told I haven't been strict enough." Frau Messner sighed and shook her head. "I admit that Johanna has been so helpful, I forget sometimes she is here to be disciplined. So for the past two days she has gone without meals and . . . she's cleaning toilets."

I knew that Gertrude and Rikka had something to do with this. "Johanna is a wonderful person. She works hard, and the children love her. Why does she have to be disciplined?"

Frau Messner gave me a long look. I could not tell if she was angry with me for asking, or if she were sorrowful. "Gertrude and Rikka put her to the test—and she failed. She will not capitulate."

"What kind of test? Who gave them the right to test Johanna?" I demanded.

"They tried forcing her to sign the form renouncing her religion."

"Of course Johanna wouldn't give in. She is loyal to her own beliefs. That is why she is trustworthy in everything. You know that, Frau Messner."

"*Ja,* what you say is true. I trust her with anything here in Lebensborn. However, I am supposed to be training her to be a loyal German," Frau Messner said, "and I was recently told that I have failed in my duty."

"But Johanna is a loyal German," I argued. "She obeys the law and she is kind. Her people do not start riots or cause dissension. They do not lie or steal. Johanna is loving and clean and polite and . . . a lot better than most people." I could hear the anger rising in my own voice, and I noticed Gertrude turn and look my way.

"Johanna is a tower of strength and yes, she is a good person." Frau Messner looked down at her hands, which she clutched tightly. "However, she cannot win, don't you see?"

"I heard Herr Himmler is coming here today."

"*Ja,* Reichsführer Himmler is coming to celebrate his birthday and to give a present to any child born on October seventh." Frau Messner glanced nervously around the room. "And I would like to keep Johanna out of sight."

Suddenly Gertrude and Rikka approached, obviously having overheard Frau Messner's words. "*Ja,* Wendy, you should be honored. You're going to meet Reichsführer Himmler in person," said Rikka.

"It would be an even greater honor for Johanna!" Gertrude said with a laugh.

"Ja," Rikka agreed smoothly. "Johanna must meet Reichsführer Himmler. He's sure to be interested in her progress."

I knew immediately what Gertrude and Rikka had in mind. Johanna would be required to salute Reichsführer Himmler and say "Heil Hitler" when he entered. They would be delighted to see Johanna punished even more.

"Johanna is not here," Frau Messner told them.

Rikka spoke up in a loud voice. She rattled off something in fast German, and I couldn't keep up with her. My knowledge of the language was limited, and Rikka knew that. She was deliberately keeping me out of the conversation. I turned and walked away. I wished I could warn Johanna that Gertrude and Rikka were setting a trap.

I spent the morning with the new babies. It was interesting and emotional to meet the young mothers—not much older than I—who had given birth to babies they might never know. One mother, Elise, was almost seventeen. Her blond hair spread out over the pillow and caught rays of the sun from the window. She seemed childlike and small herself as she lay there on the bed, asleep.

Elise had a baby boy, and my job was to talk to her and help her as she regained consciousness from the anesthesia she was given. "Elise," I said softly. "You've had a baby boy, and you both have done very well."

"Did you say I had a boy?" she asked sleepily.

"Yes. I peeked at him in the nursery. He is beautiful."

"Is he blond?"

"Well, he's practically bald right now." I laughed a little. "But believe me; he's very cute with a little turned-up nose."

"He's healthy?"

"He's strong and healthy—with a very loud cry."

Elise gave a little laugh. "Will I be able to keep him?"

"I'm not sure, Elise. He belongs to Germany now, doesn't he?"

Elise didn't answer. She closed her eyes, and I assumed she was asleep again, until I saw a tear slip down her cheek. Then she whispered, "Yes, he belongs to Germany."

After lunch the staff was busy cleaning up crumbs from the table and sweeping the floor. I sat in a chair and blew up balloons until I was dizzy. Rikka and Gertrude tied my balloons to chairs around the table. One of the kitchen staff set a large cake, decorated with white frosting and pink and white flowers, in the center of the table. Someone else brought in a punch bowl filled with pink juice and scoops of vanilla ice cream.

The doorbell rang, and I looked up, expecting to see Herr Himmler stride into the room. Instead a familiar blond woman came in carrying a little boy. The child was dressed in a tiny German uniform complete with the shiny brass buttons, an officer's hat, and the swastika armband. As his mother set him down, he immediately extended his right arm in a salute. "Heil Hitler!"

Everyone in the room clapped, laughed, and answered, "Heil Hitler." The boy looked around at his audience and smiled proudly. Then he caught sight of me. "Wen-dee! Wen-dee!" he cried, running to me with his arms outstretched.

"Hunfrid!" I gathered him into my arms and kissed his little cheeks until his hat fell off.

"I . . . a big boy soldier, Wendy," he said in German. "Why you crying?" He struggled out of my arms and once again saluted. "Heil Hitler!" He waited for me to respond, but I could not. I knew everyone was watching, but I still could not salute. This little Polish boy, whose mother was murdered, was now one of Hitler's children.

No one seemed to notice that I did not return the salute. Fortunately for me, Rikka and Gertrude were not in the room, for they surely would have made an issue out of it.

I soon found out that Gertrude and Rikka had gone to find Johanna and bring her to the party. They were now standing in the dining-room entrance. Johanna stood between them. She was dressed in a plain gray uniform and on her chest was a patch—a purple triangle, the symbol the Bible Students were required to wear.

Gertrude shoved Johanna into the room. "We thought Johanna would love to meet Reichsführer Himmler today."

32
Johanna's Ordeal

Gertrude's shove was so strong, Johanna nearly fell as she lurched into the room.

Instinctively, I ran to help her, but Rikka pushed me aside.

Frau Messner shouted, "Gertrude and Rikka, who told you to bring Johanna here today?"

"We felt it was our duty, and I discussed it with my mother. She wondered how Johanna was doing, since she arranged for Johanna to work here. I have already explained to my mother that you have not been disciplining Johanna and you have made her more of a 'trusted employee' than a prisoner. My mother gave me permission to come here and see just what is going on. After all, my mother . . ."

"I know very well the authority your mother has here—as a doctor," Frau Messner said wearily, "but she does not have authority over my treatment of Johanna."

"You can tell her that when you see her," Gertrude said haughtily, "which will be very soon. You can be sure of that."

Ordinarily, I would not be able to understand all this in my limited German. However, in her anger and arrogance, instead of her usual rush of words, Gertrude spoke slowly, clearly, and brazenly.

"Johanna most certainly is treated as a prisoner," Frau Messner stated. "She has no freedom outside of this facility. Because of the way you trapped her this week, she has had no food for several days and she has been cleaning toilets with her bare hands. Now you are planning to make more trouble for her—as well as for all of us. No one appointed you to be her judge or jailer."

Before the discussion could go on further, the front door opened and two officers strode in. I recognized one of them immediately. He wore spectacles and had a haughty smile on his face—just as in the posters plastered all over Berlin and in the newspapers. It was Reichsführer Heinrich Himmler. I heard it whispered that he had also created the death camps.

"Heil Hitler," he shouted, and his right hand swept out like the blade of a bayonet.

"Heil Hitler!" came replies from around the room.

Apparently, Herr Himmler did not notice the three girls on the other side of the room—including the one in the middle who did not salute.

Before someone could notice or mention Johanna's refusal to salute, Hunfrid diverted everyone's attention by suddenly scampering into the center of the group. Standing straight, once again he shot his arm into a perfect salute. "Heil Hitler!" he shouted, grinning proudly.

His new parents did not lose much time, teaching him his patriotic duty to the Führer, I thought.

Herr Himmler shook Hunfrid's little hand and spoke in rapid German. I prayed that Hunfrid's salute and uniform took attention away from Johanna.

Frau Messner motioned toward Elise, who was in a wheelchair, holding her baby. After introductions, Herr Himmler presented her with a package elegantly wrapped with a silver bow. Then, glancing around, as if to make sure everyone was watching, he gathered the baby into his arms and kissed him on the head. A newspaper photographer snapped pictures of the baby, who was now a godson to the Reichsführer.

Elise opened the package and held up the silver cup for all to see. After she spoke a few prepared words of gratitude, everyone applauded then sat down at the decorated table to enjoy cake and tea—everyone, that is, except Johanna.

The Reichsführer stood up and, noticing Johanna, who stood silently and awkwardly nearby, motioned to her with his hand. She walked to his side and curtsied. "*Guten Morgen,* Herr Reichsführer."

"Who are you and why are you not joining us?" he asked. Then, noticing the purple triangle patch on her uniform, he said, "Oh, I see. You are a stubborn *Bibelforscher*—one of those who defy our Führer and the laws of the Third Reich. What is your name?"

"My name is Johanna Thalberg, sir," she answered.

"And what are you doing here?"

"I have been assigned to help Frau Messner with the children."

Frau Messner explained. "Lebensborn is considered her reeducation facility, Herr Reichsführer. She has been a valuable asset here. She speaks several languages—she's very bright and—"

"Never mind how brilliant she is," Himmler interrupted with a frown. "Has she been reeducated? Has she signed a renouncement of her religion?"

I saw Rikka nudge Gertrude, who smiled and nodded, and a rush of anger flashed over me. Those two cold-blooded witches were actually having fun, eager to see what kind of cruelty Johanna would suffer now.

Frau Messner clasped her hands. "I'm sorry to say she has not signed her document of renouncement."

"How is she being punished?"

"For the past two days she has been without food and assigned to bathroom duty."

"And did she yield today?"

Frau Messner was flustered and embarrassed. "I have not had time to speak with her today. And those girls brought her up here just now . . . without my consent." She gave Rikka and Gertrude a withering look.

Herr Himmler turned to Johanna and leaned toward her threateningly. "Have you thought about your duties and loyalty to our Fatherland?"

Johanna nodded. "Yes, sir, and I have always attended to my duties to my Fatherland. However, I have a stronger loyalty to my God and his Kingdom. I cannot sign that document." She closed her eyes for a moment, and I wondered if she were praying. "I cannot Heil Hitler, and I will not renounce my heavenly father."

The Reichsführer's face reddened. "We have been patient with you long enough, *Fräulein*. I will see to it that you are removed from this facility and sent to a place where you will get the discipline you need." Then he paused, as if trying to remember something. "What did you say your name is?"

"Johanna Thalberg."

Herr Himmler waited for a moment. Then he said, "Thalberg. A good German name, and you and your family have corrupted it." He stroked his nose. "Do you have a brother, Eric?"

"Yes, sir."

"Well, he would not capitulate, either. And he paid the price this week." Herr Himmler had a slight smile on his face. "He was executed yesterday."

I held both my hands over my mouth to keep myself from crying out.

Johanna's face paled, and she staggered as if about to faint, but she was able to grab ahold of the table. After a moment she was able to speak. "I am proud of Eric. He was able to stand loyal to God. He will be rewarded with life again."

"You . . . dumm . . . ," The Reichsmarschall sputtered, at

a loss for words. "Your foolish brother was a traitor to our Führer . . . and to the Fatherland. He would not become a soldier; he would not salute; he would not join the youth group—he was given enough time."

Johanna spoke up. "With all due respect, sir, neither my brother nor I are traitors. We are good citizens and always uphold the laws of the land that are in accord with God's laws, which tell us to love our enemies. My brother would not kill anyone."

Once again Herr Himmler wiped his nose with his finger. "He was German! He could have lived if he had signed a simple document and gone off to war with other young men!"

I wanted to scream out, *Oh, Johanna, just sign the document! Do anything. Lie. Do not argue with this man. He'll certainly kill you, too.*

The Reichsmarschall was angry to the point of trembling. He put out his hand and, with his finger, he made a slash across Johanna's throat. "You will lose your head—just like your brother did."

I could feel nausea coming up into my mouth, and I began to feel wobbly. I was more horrified and frightened than I had been on the U-boat with bombs exploding around us.

Johanna stood firm and yet was respectful. "I hope that I will be as faithful as Eric. You see, sir, I know that should we die, God has the power to remember us and give us life again in his Kingdom."

Reichsführer Himmler wiped his nose with his

finger—again. He then turned to those in the room who watched in silence. "I have heard all this before. Our Führer says this brood of *Bibelforscher* will be destroyed—like bugs." He flicked his hand as if swatting a fly. Then he swung around to Johanna. "See how you spoiled what was to be a lovely celebration?" He called to the other officer who stood by the window. "Get her out of here. I'll deal with her later."

The officer grabbed Johanna by the arm and propelled her across the room. At that moment little Hunfrid, in his soldier's uniform, scurried after them. *"Nein! Nein!"* He banged his tiny fists on the soldier's legs. "Halt!"

The soldier reached down and angrily pushed Hunfrid aside.

My favorite little boy sat on the floor and sobbed. "Yo-Yo." His name for Johanna. The soldier took Johanna out of the room to . . . where? A death camp? *Would I ever see her again?* I wondered as the door closed behind them.

I had to get away. I flung my bag over my shoulder, pushed through the onlookers, and raced across the room, out the front door, and onto the street.

33
Desperate

I ran down the sidewalk and crossed the street, not waiting for the light to change, while horns beeped at me and someone yelled from a truck window. I did not care.

When I saw an empty bus bench under the sheltering branches of an oak tree, I fell onto it, breathless from crying and sick from the terrible scene I had left behind. I had forgotten my coat and sat shivering on the bench.

My sweet friend Johanna would certainly be sent to a camp—and probably to the same fate as her brother. That man—that cruel Himmler—seemed elated to break the news of Eric's horrible death by slicing his finger across Johanna's neck.

What will Adrie say when she comes to pick me up and hears how I ran out of Lebensborn this morning? She will give me a lecture about Johanna and how traitors deserve their fate.

I looked around and spotted a public telephone booth nearby. Johanna and Barret were the only two people I could confide in. I needed to talk to Barret. I fumbled through my shoulder bag and found the scribbled paper with Barret's number. I went to the telephone, put in the coins I needed, dialed, and waited.

"Hallo!" Barret's voice.

"It's me, Wendy."

"Ah, Wendy Vendy! What a surprise! Where are you?"

I began to cry again.

"What's wrong? Tell me."

"Himmler—he is at Lebensborn—and he took Johanna away. Barret, they killed her brother."

"Oh, I'm sorry. Johanna must be heartbroken." He was silent for a moment. "I hate to say this, but . . . It would happen sooner or later, Wendy. She is a *Bibelforscher*, after all. They were the first Christian group that Hitler banned and the most widely and severely persecuted. So it's to be expected that Johanna would eventually be imprisoned."

"There is nothing anyone can do, is there?" I asked.

"The *Bibelforscher* already in the prison will encourage her. She will be among her friends."

I heaved a sigh. "I don't want to go back to Lebensborn. Adrie will be waiting, and when she finds out how I reacted to Johanna's arrest—"

Barret listened and then spoke slowly. "Go back. Act as if nothing happened—or as if you don't care."

"But I do care. Everyone knows I love Johanna."

"You are honest, and you show your feelings. However, here in Germany you must be cautious with your words. You are no longer a little girl, my Wendy Vendy. Living here makes us grow up quickly—to survive. Even if you are horrified with what is going on here, you need to pretend all is well. Remember, though, that you do not need to pretend with me. You and I will keep our own secrets."

I felt a warm tingle as if it came right from the phone. "I hope to see you soon, but I wonder if Adrie is suspicious of my walks to the park."

"Then we'll find another place to meet. I don't want to stop seeing you . . . and Watcher, of course." He laughed softly.

"I don't want to stop seeing you, either," I said.

"Will Adrie be at Lebensborn to pick you up soon?"

I looked at my watch. "Yes. In about a half hour." I paused, trying to think how I should approach Adrie. "I'll pretend to be a true German and say, 'It's too bad Johanna didn't sign her paper and go free.'"

"*Ja, gut!* That should stop any more conversation on the subject of Johanna. Don't be emotional or angry. Pretend you have accepted the situation with Johanna."

"I will, but it won't be easy."

"We'll talk more tomorrow at the park. Meanwhile, be careful."

I hung up just as the coin fell into the box. After wiping my nose and the last of my tears, I headed back to Lebensborn.

As I approached the building, I noticed Adrie's car in

the drive where Reichsführer Himmler's car had been parked. At least he was gone and I would not have to see his stupid, simpering face—or watch him pick his nose.

I checked my watch and realized that Adrie was early. Someone must have called her. Would she be furious with me for causing a scene by running out? I could never tell for sure what Adrie's response would be.

I went up to the door and was about to ring the bell when I realized my hands were trembling. The sick, icy chill I felt earlier as they dragged Johanna away had returned. I took a deep breath and rang the bell. *Pretend. Pretend.* I told myself.

Almost immediately Frau Messner opened the door, her large form a dark shadow in the doorway. Without a word she stood aside and Adrie peered out.

"Wendy, wherever did you go?" Adrie asked uneasily in English.

"I took a walk."

"You didn't take your coat, and it's cold out there. Why didn't you tell anyone where you were going?" Adrie reached out, took my hand, pulling me into the foyer. "Come in and let everyone see that you're all right."

I drew back. "No, Adrie. I want to go home. Now."

A look of dismay darkened Adrie's eyes. She turned to Frau Messner and spoke regretfully in German. "Wendy's not feeling well. I'm taking her home straightaway."

Frau Messner nodded. "She did have a difficult day." She handed my coat to Adrie.

Rikka and Gertrude were standing nearby, watching

me with shaking smiles as if they were about to burst into laughter.

"Don't you want to say good-bye to the other girls?" Adrie suggested in English as she reached into her purse for her keys. "Surely, you should at least apologize."

"Apologize? For what?" I demanded. I looked directly Gertrude and Rikka, who stood behind Adrie. *"Rohlinge!"* The German for "cruel brutes" came out of somewhere in my brain. I spit the word in a loud whisper at their leering faces, and then stomped down the stairs and out to the car.

Still shaking from anguish over Johanna's arrest, I waited for Adrie. I could hear her say something in a soothing voice to Frau Messner before she followed me to the car.

Without a word, I climbed into the passenger's seat. Adrie started the car and backed out into the street. I dreaded the drive home.

34
The Ride Home

For a short while, neither Adrie nor I said anything. Part of me wanted to tell her how sad I was. I wanted to ask her if she could help Johanna. I needed a mom who would understand, who would love me, and who would make everything all right—like my mom back in New York.

I knew, though, that the most important person in Adrie's life was not me. It was Adolf Hitler.

Adrie finally spoke. "Do you want to tell me what happened today?"

"You know already, don't you?"

"Only what I heard from Frau Messner—that Johanna was taken away by Reichsführer Himmler." Adrie shook her head. "She told me that you ran out of the building in tears."

"You heard right."

"How do you feel about this? About Johanna?"

"Johanna was . . . is . . . a good friend, a good person, a good German." I realized it was not easy to pretend after all.

Adrie drew a deep breath. "No, she's not a good German."

I sat up straight in my seat. "There are criminals who steal, who cheat, who murder . . . but they will salute Hitler. Who is the better German—the criminals who disobey the law? Or some quiet, kind person like Johanna, who only asks for her right to worship God first?"

Adrie was silent for a long time, thinking. Then she said, "If everyone believed as Johanna and those Bible Students, no one would fight, and we'd lose the war."

"If everyone believed as she does, there would be no war." I turned my face to the window. "What those two girls did was unforgivable. They set the whole thing up just to see Johanna taken away."

"You knew girls like that in Maine—the Crystals. They were cruel to you."

"That's true," I admitted. "But they didn't send me away to be killed."

"What do you mean? No one is going to kill Johanna."

"No? Herr Himmler told her she'd die like her brother—with her head cut off!"

We were almost home when she said, "You have the wrong attitude. You don't put the Third Reich first in your life."

"Of course I don't. I'm not your perfect, Aryan, German maiden."

"I don't expect you to be perfect."

"I can't believe in or trust in the kind of government that is murdering thousands of Jews every day."

Adrie bristled. "Wherever did you get that idea?"

"I've heard it . . . from lots of people."

Adrie put her foot on the brake, and the car squealed as she pulled up to the sidewalk and stopped. Then turning to me, she said angrily, "I want you to tell me right now where you ever heard such a thing."

I was suddenly fearful of Adrie. I would never tell her that Johanna confided in me. I certainly could not tell her that Opa and Barret had told me it was true. "I . . . I don't know where I heard it. Just talk."

"It was Johanna, wasn't it?"

"She told me how her people were being killed."

"Her people deserve to die. They are traitors!" Adrie's voice rose.

"Is it true or not?" I demanded. "Are thousands of Jews being killed every day?"

She didn't answer for a moment. Then she sputtered. "S-sometimes I feel like sending *you* to a disciplinary school to Germanize you. Maybe then *you'd* learn to see the good things our Führer has promised for our Fatherland."

I felt as if a knife had stabbed me. I folded my arms across my chest to stop the pain. "You don't mean that, Adrie, do you?" I asked, tears brimming again. "You're my mother. Would you really send me away to one of those places?"

Adrie sighed, rolled her eyes, and then shook her head. "No. I only want what is best for you."

"Then let's not talk about this anymore. Please. Can we just go home? All I want in this whole world tonight is to climb into bed and hug my dog."

To my surprise, Adrie reached out and touched my face. "I do love you, Wendy. I realize you are not German. That is my fault, for letting you live in the States. The only thing I want in this world is for us to be together and believe in the same cause."

"Adrie, you just told me that no one is going to kill Johanna. If that is so, is there anything you can do to guarantee that? Is there some way you can get her out of the camp?"

Adrie looked into my eyes for a long time, then turned away, started up the car, and began driving again. "I can't do anything to help her."

We drove along in silence until we reached our driveway. Adrie then slammed on the brakes and turned to me. "And I wouldn't do anything, even if I could."

35
The Three of Us

I had a terrible headache that night. Yet, as sad and disturbed as I was, I fell asleep as soon as Watcher climbed onto my bed and snuggled against my legs. I did not want to think about Johanna—I knew I would stay awake all night if I allowed myself to remember everything that happened that day.

Yet I could not get away from my dreams. I saw Herr Himmler with his sickening smirk. He hovered over me like a grimacing ogre—an evil man despite all his adoring fans.

Then I was back in Maine with my friend Jill Winters. She and I were sitting on the floor by the radio, listening to her famous father sing "The White Cliffs of Dover."

In my dream Adrie called out, "Turn off that radio! Anyone listening to that music will be put to death!"

I woke up, shaking. My headache was pounding, and

now my throat was sore. I reached out for Watcher, who was sleeping at the foot of my bed. "Come here, boy," I whispered.

He crawled closer, and I put my arm around him, falling back into a restless sleep.

The next morning, Thursday, Watcher and I were up before Adrie left for work at the *Abwehr* office. When we went downstairs, she was sipping coffee at the dining-room table with the newspaper spread out before her. "Frieda has a special breakfast for you this morning," she said to me.

"Why? Does she know everything that happened yesterday?"

Adrie looked up. "Well, I told her some of it. She could tell you had been crying when you came home."

I went into the kitchen and let Watcher out into the yard. Frieda turned and smiled as she cracked an egg into a bowl and began whipping batter.

Adrie followed me. "What are you going to do today, Wendy?"

"I don't know. I'll take my dog for a walk, I guess." I stayed at the open door, waiting for Watcher to come back. I could not see Adrie, but I could feel her penetrating gaze as I tried to be cheerful. My head was still pounding, and it hurt to swallow. I did not want to tell her. She would stay home, or get me to a doctor. I wanted to see Barret.

Adrie put her cup into the sink and announced, "I've got to go to work. We are still looking for those White Rose members. It was bad enough that they distributed their pamphlets secretly. Now I hear they are painting their messages on walls and buildings."

"Why are you so worried about the White Rose?" I asked casually. "No one pays attention to what a few college kids are saying, do they?"

"We can't have our own people undermining our war efforts and saying slanderous things against our Führer." Adrie took a small mirror from her pocket, checked her hair, and turned to me again. "I must go back to Munich for a few days. I hope you are well enough to be left alone again. After your reaction to what happened to Johanna, I'm worried about you."

"I'm not alone. Frieda is here."

"You'll feel better once you go back to Lebensborn and face those girls who exposed Johanna. If they start in on you, let them see you do not give a hoot about them. Then they'll stop harassing you." Adrie picked up her briefcase from a nearby chair and headed for the door. "You should have done that with those girls in Maine. Instead you fell apart."

"I'm not the same girl I was when I visited Maine."

"Well, that's a good thing. See? Living here has made you a better and stronger person." Adrie looked pleased as she went out the door.

"Yes, I am stronger," I answered.

Frieda did make a special American breakfast—hot cakes with sweet syrup and lots of butter and thick slices of ham. I sank down at the kitchen table and allowed her to wait on me—even to tuck a napkin into the neck of my pajamas.

The syrup felt good on my sore throat, but it was hard to swallow the ham. And even though the pancakes were soft, I could only manage to eat half of one.

"*Danke,* Frieda," I said, pushing the plate away.

Frieda looked at me with concern. Then she came around the table, put her arms around me, and kissed me on the cheek.

At her gentleness and affection, the tears came spilling out over my lashes and dribbled down my face, as if a dam had broken. I clung to Frieda and trembled as she held me. Adrie must have told her yesterday's events at Lebensborn. It did not matter how Adrie may have told the story, all I needed was that hug and that show of affection.

Later I was eager to get to the park, where I hoped Barret was waiting, but I walked slowly. My head pounded with each step. Watcher tugged and whined. He wanted to see Barret too.

Barret was already there with his white cane, sitting by the fountain. I hurried over and sat down next to him. "I knew you were here because Watcher was so excited."

Barret reached out and grabbed both of my hands. "Wendy Vendy, how are you?" he asked. "I've been worried about you. You were so distressed when we talked yesterday."

"Barret, yesterday was the worst day of my life. I have never witnessed anything so cruel—not even in the scariest movies. Johanna says the Bible teaches us to love one another, including our enemies, and she stayed respectful even when Himmler said they had beheaded her brother. What an ugly monster of a man." Once again the tears welled up in my eyes. "I'll . . . probably never see her again."

Barret could not see my tears, but he had to have heard the distress in my voice, because he pulled me closer and put his arm around my shoulders. "Wendy Vendy," he whispered, using his teasing name for me. "You are like a little sister—innocent and trusting. You have never been conditioned to circumstances like these."

I leaned against him. He felt strong and warm. "Why are the Bible Students hated so much?"

"One reason is that their magazines are distributed all over the world, exposing what is going on here."

"Do you think Johanna has been killed?"

"Honestly, we may never know." Barrett seemed thoughtful, then asked, "Have you heard about the White Rose? They are speaking out too, in their own way."

"Yes. Adrie told me about them. She said they will be caught and punished."

To my surprise, Barret bent over and took off his shoe. Inside was a folded paper, which he pulled out and handed to me. "This is one of their leaflets. Opa read it to me."

"Having that paper is dangerous, Barret," I warned, my voice a hoarse whisper. "Suppose someone found it on you."

"They'd know I couldn't read it." He laughed, and then said seriously, "But it wouldn't matter. If I were caught with this, they'd suspect me—blind or not." He whispered in my ear. "I wanted you to see there are Germans who are willing to speak up, even though they do so anonymously. Once you have read this, burn it immediately."

"I'll be careful." I took off my own shoe and tucked the folded leaflet inside. Then I sat back and faced my friend. "Barret, I want to leave Germany. I want to go home—back to the States. Opa said he'd help me."

Barret nodded and looked sad. "*Ja*, but if you go away, Wendy, I'll be very lonely."

"You can come too! We'll go together. We will find the way out of Germany. Watcher will come with us. As long as we have each other, we can do it."

Barret took a long sigh, and then shook his head. "I would be a burden."

"Barret, I have to have hope. Please do not tell me it's impossible. I need to believe there is a way out. Go along with my dream. Even if it never happens, it's comforting to pretend there is a way. We'll make plans for the three of us. I will not go without you—even in my pretend world. We will all go together."

Watcher seemed excited, because he jumped up from the cement, put his front paws on Barret's knees, and licked his face.

"See? Watcher knows that the three of us can do anything!" I put my arm around Barret and hugged him. Then I whispered. "Barret, I must go home now. I'm not feeling well. My head is pounding and my throat is sore."

"It's no wonder, after what you went through yesterday." He reached for his cane and stood up. "Go home and get rested."

"Adrie will be away, so I'll see you here on Saturday."

We walked to the sidewalk then turned in opposite directions. Watcher looked after Barret, as if undecided with whom he should go. I gave him a tug. "Let's go home, Watcher."

The walk home seemed longer than usual. I felt hot and weak. When we reached the entrance at the back of our house, I was relieved to find the gate unlatched. We went inside and up to the terrace where Frieda was sitting at a table, drinking tea and reading mail.

"Frieda!" I called. I did not recognize my own voice. "Frieda!"

She looked up, puzzled, and then came to me. "Are you all right?" she asked in German.

"I'm so ill," I whispered. "It hurts to talk . . . and my head . . ."

Frieda put her arm around my waist and felt my forehead with the inside of her other wrist. "You are burning up."

I felt myself my legs give out—and Frieda holding me. I knew I was about to faint.

My shoe! *What if someone finds the White Rose paper in my shoe?*

It was too late. I dropped into a deep hole of blackness.

36
Lost Time

Where am I? I am deep in the sea—with icy water on my face and neck. I am turning over repeatedly in the waves. Shivering. So cold.

I hear echoing voices far away. They are speaking German. I can't understand. Is it Johanna? What have they done with Johanna?

I try to call out. "Adrie! Frieda!" My voice is garbled.

A man is speaking. He is forcing my mouth open. Get away from me. Are you Himmler? Do not take Johanna!

Now . . . I feel cool facecloths and comforting words. Is it Mommy? My mommy in New York? Am I in New York? Is that my daddy holding my hand?

I miss you, Daddy and Mommy. Please come for me.

Over the next several weeks—or so I found out later—I was in a dark place, not knowing much of anything. Night and day dragged into one long nightmare. At times I knew I was in my room. Other times I thought I was back in Maine, or in New York. How disappointing when I realized I was still in Berlin.

I was often aware of Frieda sitting me up in my bed, fluffing pillows, coaxing me to swallow the soft food she made for me—scrambled eggs, chicken soup, oatmeal. I was afraid to swallow because of the pain. I dreaded to hear footsteps coming toward my room, because I knew someone would be forcing me to eat and drink.

One morning Adrie brought water with ice cubes and a straw to sip. "You must have fluids, Wendy. You are severely dehydrated."

I could barely speak. "No. Please."

"If you don't drink, we will have to feed you with a tube down your throat. I will have a nurse come and force you to eat. You don't want that, do you?" Adrie held the straw to my mouth, and I tried to sip—just the smallest amount—to satisfy her.

"Shards of broken glass," I whispered, pointing to my throat.

"It's time we called the doctor again. He has been here several times, but you probably don't remember."

"What did he say?"

"You have an infected throat. He coated your tonsils with iodine. You must remember that. You put up a big fuss."

I shook my head.

Adrie left the room, and I could hear her speaking on

the telephone in her bedroom. The overhead bedroom light was harsh and bright, and my eyes hurt; there was also the unbearable headache. My head pounded with every sound—squirrels quarreling in the big tree outside my window; dogs barking; telephones ringing; doors shutting.

"The doctor is coming," she said later, peering into my room. "I'm staying home again today. I cannot go back to Munich when you are so ill."

"Johanna?" I tried to ask about Johanna, but it hurt too much.

"She is gone" was all that Adrie said.

Frieda came into the room and spoke softly in German to Adrie. It was an effort for me to translate what they were saying. I wanted to hear only English.

The doctor came. He forced my mouth open again, looked down with a light, then shook his head and spoke seriously to Adrie. I turned away and prayed they wouldn't poke at my throat again.

Suddenly someone shoved a rubber mask onto my face, and I smelled the sickening sweet scent of gas. I slipped back, deep into that strange sea where dreams and reality all melded together.

Hours? Days later? I woke up in the bright light of my bedroom and was shocked to realize that I could not move. I was strapped to the bed with bands of heavy material. Was I being punished for something? Had they found the secret paper in my shoe?

However, my throat wasn't quite as sore now. I could

open my mouth wider without as much pain, and I could breathe more easily.

Adrie peeked in, and seeing me awake, gestured for Frieda to come in. Frieda smiled at me gently—sadly—and held up a bottle of medicine and a spoon.

Frieda plumped up the pillows as Adrie loosened the bands that held me tightly to the bed. Then they lifted me to a sitting position. If it would make me better, I was more than willing to take the new drug, so I opened my mouth while Adrie fed me a tablespoonful of the strange-tasting medicine. It didn't hurt as much to swallow now.

"You must take this medicine every four hours. It's the new miracle sulfonamide drug, Prontosil from Bayer—made here in Germany of course. The allies do not have this. You are very fortunate that there is still some available. Most of it is being used for our wounded soldiers."

"What's wrong with me?" I croaked.

"Your sore throat turned into quinsy throat—it produced a large abscess behind your tonsil. It's no wonder you couldn't swallow. The doctor gave you anesthesia and pierced the boil."

"What has happened in the war? Did the Russians surrender?" I was hoping the war was over—no matter who won.

"Things are not good for our troops at Stalingrad."

"So the Germans have not surrendered yet?"

"Of course not. They'll die before they'd surrender."

I tried to get comfortable. "Take those straps off me, please," I whispered to Adrie.

"No, the restraints will keep you from falling. We have to be sure the anesthesia wears off first. Just go to sleep." She turned off the overhead bedroom light and left on the small bedroom lamp by my bed. It gave a soft, comforting glow, and for the first time I believed I would get better.

I closed my eyes. Time for me had stopped. How long had it been since I had seen Barret? Was he worried about me? Did he know I'd been ill?

What about my shoe? Surely, someone must have found the White Rose brochure folded up inside by now. Who? Adrie? No, she would have been so angry, I would have heard about it, no matter how sick I might have been. I had to look for it! I struggled under the straps, then realized I was too weak to get up. I sank back onto the pillow and tried to remember.

When I came home ill that day, Frieda had undressed me and put me to bed. If she had discovered the brochure, would she have told Adrie? Or had she even found it, considering how frightened she was when I fainted? Could the paper still be in my shoe?

37
Recuperation

After several more weeks I was able to get up and walk around a bit with Adrie's or Frieda's help. My legs were rubbery, and it was hard to keep my balance. Once I was alone, the first thing I did was to look in my closet for the shoes I had worn that day in the park. They were there, on the shoe rack. I held my breath as I looked inside each shoe. There was nothing there. Someone must have removed the White Rose brochure.

I could not imagine Adrie finding it and not exploding at me. The only other persons who had come into my room were Frieda . . . and the doctor. The doctor would have no reason to look in my shoes. Had Frieda found that folded paper? If so, had she read it? Perhaps she just tossed it out without even looking at it. Should I ask her? Did I dare bring it up? The anxiety I felt made my headache started throbbing again. I went to the bed and dropped back onto the sheets.

Later that day the doctor came and told Adrie my blood was thin—whatever that meant—and he prescribed iron and vitamins for me to take every day.

"You have been seriously ill for more than a month," Adrie said. "So it will take several months to recuperate before you're back to normal." She sighed. "That means you cannot go back to Lebensborn—or to school, for that matter. I was hoping you'd be going to school, at least. But you need to stay quiet and rest here at home."

I was so relieved, my eyes filled with tears.

"Oh, I know that makes you unhappy," Adrie said sympathetically, noticing my tears.

She had no idea how delighted I was. Why, it was worth being sick to know I would not have to go back to Lebensborn. I wouldn't need to attend a school, either. Now Adrie would go back to Munich and I would be able to meet Barret again.

Frieda helped me down the stairs to supper that night. We celebrated my first time downstairs since I became ill. We ate in the dining room. Adrie lit candles, and we each had a little glass of wine.

"*Prost!*" Adrie said, lifting her glass. "Here's to good health for all of us—especially Wendy." Then she added, "You don't remember much of what happened when you were so sick, but I was headed to Munich. Once I talked with the doctor, I canceled my trip to stay with you."

"Oh, I'm sorry I caused you to postpone your trip, Adrie," I said.

"It wasn't your fault, of course! However, that week Munich was bombed badly. So perhaps you saved my life, Wendy."

"I'm thankful you weren't there," I said.

Frieda had made my favorite: pot roast and vegetables. "Eat lots of meat," she said. "It will build your blood."

We ate quietly, with Watcher at my feet, when Adrie suddenly spoke up. "Oh, I must tell you something else, now that you are better. I spotted that watcher in the woods twice since you have been ill. Both times it was in the morning. I've decided I will call the police tomorrow and tell them to capture this person once and for all."

I looked down at my plate so my eyes wouldn't give away my apprehension. I was certain it was Opa. "Do you have any idea who it might be?"

"No. I wasn't concerned before, but this has been going on for too long."

Has Opa been spying on our house to see what has happened to me? He must stop. I've got to let him know I am all right.

Later that evening Watcher and I sat with Adrie in her office while Berlin radio played music by German bands and singers.

Suddenly Dr. Goebbels interrupted with an important announcement regarding the Sixth Army on the Eastern Front. His high-pitched fanatical voice screamed out to German citizens. "Our gallant soldiers are closing in on Stalingrad! Victory is near. Their most dangerous enemy is the winter weather. Our troops need warm clothing and boots. Bring your coats—especially fur coats—to our booths around the city, and we will send them to our brave men on the Eastern Front."

"I must get my furs out of storage tomorrow and bring one down to the collection place," Adrie said. "Winter is here, and you need a warm coat and jacket too. Stand up and turn around, Wendy." I did as she asked and felt uncomfortable under her critical gaze. I had seen my skinny bones and pale skin in the bathroom mirror. "Oh, Wendy. You must be at least two sizes smaller now. I am going to pick up some winter clothing for you."

"Whatever you get will be fine with me."

"That goes to show how weak you are. Usually the very thought of shopping would set you dancing." Adrie shook her head sadly. "I'll go while I'm in town tomorrow. I will be working for most of the day. Will you be all right without me? Frieda will be here."

"I'll be just fine, Adrie." My heart soared with relief. I would be able to call Barret tomorrow morning and warn him.

38
Just the Two of Us

Before Adrie went off to work the following morning, we listened to the radio and heard that Russian soldiers had surrounded the Sixth Army in Stalingrad.

"That sounds bad for the German soldiers," I commented.

"Everything will be all right. The Führer has sent Field Marshal von Manstein's soldiers to break the encirclement. Our Führer would never leave our soldiers at the hands of the Russians."

I was beginning to pay more attention to the newspaper and radio broadcasts regarding the war. I wanted to know what was happening and when and where I might go if I should try to escape. Even though it might never happen, it was a relief to know that Opa could find a way—if I really wanted to go.

I called out to Adrie as she headed for the door. "Adrie,

if you do get some clothes for me, would you pick out some warm, comfortable boots—like hiking boots?"

"Hiking boots?" she asked with an astonished look on her face. "And just where are you going hiking?"

"I think they'd be good to have for the winter. I don't want to fall or get cold." She must never know I would be walking with Barret. "One more thing, I'd really like a warm jacket with a hood. Do you think you could find one . . . with a lot of pockets?"

Adrie put her hands on her hips and shook her head. "I'm surprised you aren't begging for something chic and stylish."

"I have nowhere to go to wear chic clothes. I don't want to get sick again."

"Good for you, Wendy." Adrie smiled at me as she left.

From the window, I could see Adrie driving down to the street. Frieda was scraping dishes and pouring hot water into the sudsy dishpan. Good. While Frieda was busy, I had time to call Barret. Once upstairs, I took the phone from Adrie's room and plugged it into the phone jack in my room. Then I dialed Barret's number.

Almost immediately I heard Barret's voice. "Hallo?"

"It is me, Wendy?"

"Oh, we have been so worried, Wendy Vendy. It has been a month or more! Have you been ill? You were not feeling well the last time we were together."

"I have been very ill. I was unconscious for a long time."

"Opa tried to find out how you were. He was back in the park watching your house."

"Barret, don't let him go there again. Adrie saw him twice, and she's sending the police to set a trap."

"I'll tell him. Now that we know you're all right, he won't go near the park."

"I do have so much to tell you. Where can we meet?"

"In Opa's workshop. He has fixed up an old barn behind our apartment building. If anyone does see us, we can say we are training Watcher."

"Good. We need to train him so he can help us when we leave Germany."

"I cannot leave Opa, Wendy. Your dream cannot be mine." Barret then changed the subject. "Are you well enough to walk to the park?"

"Um, day after tomorrow—in the morning? We can meet at the park, and then you'll show me the way to Opa's workshop."

"Wednesday morning then." He hung up.

Instead of feeling happy to have spoken to Barret, I was depressed. He did not intend to leave Germany. After all, Opa and Barret were so close. What would either do without the other? I was being selfish to suggest that Barret escape with me—even if it was only a dream plan. I unplugged the phone and replaced it in Adrie's room.

In my own room, Watcher was sleeping on the rug. I knelt down and put my arms around him. "It makes me sad, but if we do go, Watcher, it will be just the two of us after all."

Watcher looked up at me drowsily, wagged his tail, and went back to sleep.

39
Princess of Secrets

It took three trips to the car to bring in all the packages of winter clothing that Adrie had purchased for me.

"I had such a good time on this shopping spree," she said, flopping down on the living-room sofa. "But it would have been more fun if you'd been with me."

"Each time you came to visit me in the States, you were loaded up with gifts and goodies," I said. "I could hardly wait for your visits."

"See? She only loves me for my money and gifts," she said in German to Frieda who was folding shopping bags.

I looked in awe at the heap of shopping bags piled on the floor. "You really bought out the store, Adrie."

Right there in the living room I tried on a pair of slacks and a sweater. "Oh, wow!" I exclaimed, clapping my hands. "I cannot believe you actually bought me slacks. My friend Jill wore slacks in the States, and it was shocking! But now, with women working in factories for the war effort, it's more acceptable and stylish."

"Actually, after your illness I decided they'd be much warmer for the winter instead of dresses."

As we opened the packages, it felt like Christmas. Adrie had purchased long-sleeved shirts and sweaters; a pleated plaid skirt with a velvet vest; a green wool coat; the sporty brown jacket with a hood and pockets I wanted; and a pair of ankle-high boots for walking or hiking.

"The boots aren't real leather, though," she apologized. "It is impossible to find real leather shoes anymore. But they should be durable."

"They are fine! Thank you."

"You're welcome."

As I tried on the boots, I wondered once again who might have found the White Rose paper in my shoe. It had been more than two months now, and no one had said a word. I looked up and saw Frieda watching me. Had she found it? Was she waiting and watching to see what I might do next? She was a loyal German, wasn't she? I'd been told not to trust anyone, not even someone kind like Frieda.

The next morning, after Adrie left, I pulled on the new coffee colored wool slacks and topped them with a soft flannel shirt and tan jacket. "I'm taking a short walk this morning," I told Frieda in German as I hitched Watcher to his leash. "I need fresh air."

She nodded. "Short walk only. Do not go far. And stay warm."

It was cold outside, and the trees had lost most of their

leaves. The few remaining were brown and crisp, and they clattered in the breeze. Sounds were clearer; car horns, sparrows chirping noisily in a hedge, a dog barking in the distance.

Watcher stopped, as if wondering where the other dog was. Then he tugged impatiently at his leash and trotted as he realized we were heading for the park.

Christmas was approaching, but there were not many decorations because of the war and out of regard for the soldiers on the Eastern Front. As I entered the park, I saw Barret by the now silent, empty fountain. "Barret!" I called, and he turned toward my voice.

Watcher caught sight of Barret and pulled away from me, his leash dragging behind him. When my dog leaped up to lick Barret's face, Barret laughed and gave Watcher a hug. Watcher then lay at Barret's feet, wiggling and whining.

"Watcher's crazy to see you," I called out as I ran toward my friend.

"I was so worried about you." He pulled me close to him. "I've missed you, Wendy Vendy," he whispered. Then he held me at arm's length. "Is it all right for you to be out walking?"

"I'm fine. The fresh, cool air feels good." I took Barret's hand and led him to a bench behind a row of evergreens, out of sight from the front entrance. Then I said, "Remember how you gave me that public letter from the White Rose group and how I tucked it away in my shoe, as you did?"

"Yes, of course. Have you read it? I hope you destroyed it."

"No. I didn't read it. As you know, I was very ill that day and in a coma—unconscious—for a long time. Weeks later, after I was recovering, I found my shoes in the closet. Barret, the brochure was gone! I have no idea where."

"Did Adrie find it? When I didn't hear from you or see you, I thought she might have discovered it and was punishing you in some way."

"If Adrie found it, she'd have been furious. If it was Frieda, she hasn't said a word. Perhaps she found the paper and just threw it out. I'm sure I can trust Frieda not to say anything to anyone."

"You cannot trust anyone, Wendy. Best friends turn on each other; neighbors are watching every move; teachers ply students with leading questions. It's not safe to rely on anyone."

"Should I ask Frieda about it?"

"Saying nothing about it is the best advice I can give you for now."

"Barret, I never did read it. Tell me what it was about?"

"It declared that the Nazi party was evil and destroying the German nation. It also said that at some point the German people would be ashamed of this era when Hitler ruled and of the evil that happened. It requested readers to pass the message on to others. However, it was nothing compared to the later brochures that revealed and spoke out against the murder of Jews." Barret blew a soft whistle. "They actually dared to say that Hitler was the child of the devil!"

"It's no wonder the group is in such danger."

We moved on to other things that had happened since we last saw each other. Later Barret, Watcher, and I walked to the apartment complex where Barret and Opa lived. He took me around to the back of the building, where a flagstone walkway led to a barn among the trees. It was a beautifully renovated outbuilding, with a red door large enough for a car to pass through. Under a large leafless tree were a bright red picnic table and benches.

Upon entering a smaller door to the right, I was surprised to see a huge, complete workshop. Tools hung neatly on the walls above long wooden counters. Windows at the back of the barn let in the afternoon sunlight. A large worktable with an overhead light above it stood in the center of the room. When Barret turned on the light, the room was as bright as day.

"This is quite a place!" I said. "Does Opa work here often?"

"Oh, yes. He loves to restore old furniture, lamps, jewelry. I often come here with him while he works."

I could picture the sweet gentle man—one of the most important figures in the Third Reich—with a cobbler's apron, happily working on a lamp or some old broken object. "He's very tidy with his tools," I observed, noticing again the variety of implements hanging on the wall.

"We keep everything in its place so I can find things more easily. We often work here together. I enjoy it because with the bright light, I can actually see some things in this room—such as those tools. They're mostly shapes, but I can tell a hammer from a hatchet when he asks me to bring him something."

"I would hope so!" I said, laughing. "You mentioned jewelry. Does Opa really work on gold and jewels?"

"Oh, yes. Even though it began as a hobby, he has become an expert. The jewelry he makes is quite beautiful. He hand-shapes silver and gold—in fact, Reichsmarschall Göring wears a ring that Opa made. The Reichsmarschall provided the stone—I think it's a diamond—and Opa structured the gold ring around it." Barret's voice became bitter. "Then Opa discovered the stone had been taken—stolen, I should say—from a Jewish victim."

"I saw Reichsmarschall Göring and his flashy rings in the newsreels back home. He looks like an arrogant buffoon!"

"He was quite a hero—an ace pilot—during the Great War," Barret went on, "and was as popular as a movie star. Now he is in charge of the Luftwaffe—the Air Force."

"He says Berlin will never be bombed or his name isn't Hermann Göring."

"Berlin was bombed in 1940," Barret reminded me, "but it didn't amount to much. However, it made Herr Göring and Hitler angry enough to blitz Britain fifty-seven nights in a row."

"The bombs will come to Berlin again. The American planes have longer ranges now. I have to get out of here before then." I sat on a chair at the worktable. "What I'd like to do is find a route for escape. I have thought of going to Bavaria. Perhaps I could discover where the secret trails are through the mountains to Switzerland." I heaved a sigh. "But I'm sure Adrie would suspect I was there and she'd find me."

"Sounds like you've already been reading and planning."

"I have! Adrie thinks I'm learning German culture, but I'm learning German geography. I've been trying to find the best and easiest way out of here."

"I thought you said this was a dream—a game you're playing."

"It's becoming more than a dream, but it is still a secret. No one knows but you."

"Well, my Princess of Secrets, I will ask Opa, 'What would be the best route?' I wouldn't be at all surprised if he knows many routes of escape."

"Please ask him. He said he'd help me." I took a deep breath. "I'm not going to beg you to come with me, but—"

"I've thought about it, Wendy," Barret cut in. "But I'm concerned that . . ."

"I know, I know. That you'd be a burden."

"That's one reason. The other is that if I did go and we were caught, they would find out I am Opa's grandson. He would be in great trouble. He does so much to help people in quiet, secretive ways. I never want him to be caught."

I felt a bit ashamed. I had almost forgotten that Opa was one of the principal men in the Third Reich. If anyone knew he helped me—or anyone else—to escape . . . I didn't want to think about the consequences.

Barret, on the other hand, thought only of his grandfather and me—never of himself. I was realizing more and more what a wonderful person Barret was and how much . . . yes . . . how much I loved him.

40
The Winter War

During December, Barrett and I were able to meet twice a week or more, and before we knew it, Christmas was here. Celebrations were subdued because of the war. People were quiet and fearful. Germans realized they could not take over Russia as easily as they had when they'd walked in and claimed Czechoslovakia, France, and Poland. The entire world was on fire with hatred and killing.

Now Operation Winter Storm, which was supposed to resupply the German troops, failed to help the Sixth Army, and General Paulus's men were without support and without supplies. Word crept out that the troops were starving and freezing to death as well as in pain and dying from their wounds. For the first time the question floated among the common people like a morning fog—silent, gray: *Could Germany possibly lose this war?* But still, it was something no one would outwardly ask.

Adrie gave me a necklace for Christmas. It had a golden heart with a ruby in the center. Engraved on the back was the word *Daughter*. I bought her a tortoise shell mirror with a matching comb and a brush trimmed in gold. Of course, the money came from Adrie, who had begun giving me an allowance. I also wrote a poem. It was hard enough to write in English; I didn't dare compose it in German. It was probably awkward, grammatically, but I hoped Adrie would like it. I printed it by hand on a white Christmas card that showed a lone deer standing in the snow with a full moon overhead.

> No matter if the world stops turning,
> Or if the moon shuts off its glow,
> Or if the sun should fade and vanish,
> Or if the tides stop in their flow.
> No matter who I am while living,
> When I am old, or should I die.
> My love for you remains forever,
> You are the rainbow in my sky.

It probably sounded mushy, and I was almost embarrassed to give it to her. Still, I needed to tell Adrie that I would always love her. Someday, if I really did leave, I hoped she would remember these words.

Adrie loved the present and she kissed the card when she read my poem.

For Frieda I bought a linen handkerchief with at least two inches of pink and white tatting around it. I remembered how my mom—Aunt Nixie—had loved tatted hankies as presents. I was surprised to see Frieda's tearful eyes when she opened the little package from me, and I wished I had given her more.

Frieda made gingerbread cookies and taught me to sing "Silent Night"—"*Stille Nacht.*" She had a deep alto voice that rang out like a church bell, and she stressed each word with feeling. I told her it did not make sense to me that warring nations sang the same Christmas carols, about peace on Earth, and yet were killing one another. Frieda did not answer. Instead she shook her head sadly and shrugged.

I never dared ask her about the brochure that I hid in my shoe.

41

White Rose Members Caught!

One Saturday, after visiting with Barrct, I discovered Adrie was back from Munich and waiting for me. "Where havc you been?" she demanded. "It's so cold. I can't imagine you staying out so long after being ill."

"That's exactly why I asked you to buy me these boots and this warm jacket." I hoped she wouldn't ask where I had been again. "So, how did everything go in Munich?"

"Very well, thank you. We caught the kids. They became too sure of themselves and were no longer careful. In fact, that girl—Sophic Scholl—gave herself and her brother away by tossing their extra bulletins from the second-floor atrium and onto the main floor of a university building. Stupid girl! The janitor saw Sophie and her brother and reported them to the police."

"Where are they and what will happen to them?"

"They are in the People's Court—*Volksgerichtshof*. They'll have a fair trial and sentence."

Frieda, who had been standing in the doorway, spoke up in German. "Who is the judge who has been appointed for their trial?"

"The presiding judge, Roland Freisler, Chief Justice of the People's Court has already been called from Berlin."

"Oh, he is very . . ." Frieda paused, searching for the right word. ". . . harsh."

"He will see that justice is done," Adrie said quickly in German to Frieda, and then in English to me. I realized Adrie was not yet sure how well I understood German.

As Frieda turned from the doorway, I saw disappointment—along with a flash of anger—cross her face.

"In other words, he is not kind," I stated. Before Adrie could answer, I left the room and headed upstairs with Watcher at my heels.

I plopped onto my big chair by the window and stared at the somber world outside.

What would happen to the White Rose students? Adrie said they would receive a just trial, but I knew they would not. Even Frieda looked upset when she heard who the judge was. He would not be compassionate to the students. Adrie practically admitted that.

I fingered the three gold monkeys on my bracelet. They reminded me of the German people who said nothing, heard nothing, and saw nothing. At least the White Rose group tried to speak out to the German people.

I thought about myself. I did not have a strong character, like Sophie Scholl or Johanna. I was upset when I saw bad things going on, but I wasn't brave enough to stand up for what was right, like they had done. I felt tears rush to my eyes, and I put my hands over my face. I was just Wendy Taylor, who liked boys, nice clothes, and going to the movies. I wanted to see no evil, hear no evil, and speak no evil.

On Saturday, Adrie was busy in her office typing up a report for the *Abwehr*. I was surprised when she told me that while she was in the university, she had met and talked with Sophie Scholl.

"What is she like?" I asked.

"Nothing special. I had a feeling she was one of them, as she seemed cautious about making new friends."

Adrie frowned. "I examined the letter so many times, I memorized the first lines: 'Nothing is so unworthy of a civilized nation as allowing itself to be "governed" without opposition by an irresponsible clique that has yielded to base instinct. It is certain that today every honest German is ashamed of his government.'" Adrie slammed her fist onto her desk. "Can you imagine? After all the Third Reich has done for Germany, these troublemakers decree it an irresponsible clique!"

"Students have a right to voice their own opinions. We had assignments back home where we had to pick some constitutional law or amendment and argue against it. It helps people to see the other side of things—"

Adrie interrupted. "Our government here—which in case you've forgotten, is your government—has proved it has God-given rights to take over Europe and bring a thousand years of power and enlightenment. Then these . . . *Scheine* . . . hand out poison to bring it down." Adrie's voice rose. "And that quote is only a miniscule part of the traitorous things they've said."

"Johanna told me that—"

"I don't want to hear anything that foolish girl told you."

I ignored her and continued. "If an organization like the White Rose or the Bible Students is from God, it can't be taken down or destroyed. If it's not from God, it will simply fall apart eventually. So why not just wait and see what happens?"

Adrie stood up and pointed to the door. "Leave. I don't want to argue with you about this." She shut the door with a slam when I left.

To my surprise, Frieda was standing in the hall wearing a troubled expression. She put a finger to her lips. *"Sei vorsichtig,"* she whispered. *Be careful.*

Adrie stayed in her office for most of the day. I heard the radio turned on, and the news was mostly about the White Rose instigators' trial tomorrow—Monday. It sounded as if they were already convicted—and I realized they did not stand a chance for a fair trial.

42
Death Trial

I slept late on Monday, February 22. As I headed down to breakfast, I passed by Adrie's office, where she was sitting at her desk. She had the radio on, and the telephone was in her hand.

"Are you expecting an important call?" I asked, hoping to set aside yesterday's argument.

"I want to hear the results of the trial with Sophie and Hans Scholl and their friend Christoph Probst. This one will be over quickly because after they found evidence—the printing press and more leaflets in Sophie's apartment—she confessed."

"What will the sentence be? Concentration camp?"

Adrie did not answer. She looked at me sideways, her eyebrows raised, as if to say, *Don't ask stupid questions.*

I pressed on. "Death?"

"Of course." The phone rang and she put her finger

to her lips. "Shh!" She turned off the radio.

I did not want to hear any more, so I left the room. I went to the kitchen, where Frieda was peeling vegetables at the sink. Watcher was asleep on his blanket under the table. He must have whined or barked during the night, and either Adrie or Frieda had let him out of my room. He looked up at me sleepily, wagged his tail, and then sank his head down on his paws again.

Frieda pushed a plate of breakfast biscuits over to me and then poured cups of tea from the kettle for both of us. I picked out one bun glazed with cinnamon, apples, and walnuts. It was so good that I helped myself to a second.

Frieda, who went back to peeling turnips and potatoes, looked over at me occasionally with serious glances. Was something bothering her? I looked to see if I had spilled tea or food onto the printed tablecloth, and brushed away a few crumbs. "Is everything all right, Frieda?" I asked in German.

Frieda opened her mouth as if to speak, but then turned away, her attention on the job at hand. *"Ja,"* she said, nodding quickly.

At that moment Adrie burst into the room. "Well, the trial is over, and all three of those students are on their way to the guillotine."

"What?" I jumped up. "Guillotine? You mean they're . . ."

"Yes." She looked at her watch. "They're dead by now, and they got exactly what they deserved. This is what happens to traitors."

"You said they'd get a fair trial."

"They d-did get a fair trial," Adrie sputtered. "They confessed, remember?"

"Confessed to what? To voicing their opinions? They were not shooting or killing anyone." I headed for the door. "There is no freedom of speech here. There's no freedom of anything here."

"Don't you dare speak of your government in that way," Adrie warned. "You'll end up at the guillotine yourself, if you keep this up."

Frieda did not look at me, but as I turned to leave, I could see her hands shaking and suddenly blood streamed from her fingers onto the vegetable peels.

"Oh, Frieda," I whispered.

She quickly tucked her bleeding fist into her apron. Her other hand she held to her mouth as if to hold back a scream.

I could not face Adrie again, so I raced up the stairs to my room and closed the door. The very thought of that brother and sister facing the guillotine just a few moments ago made me ill.

I didn't know how long I sat there. Maybe an hour. No one came to see where I was or what I was doing. Adrie didn't attempt to talk me out of my anger and shock at the outcome of the trial. She was probably tired of arguing with me or trying to make me the perfect German maiden she wanted for her daughter.

Frieda was so upset too. Was it because of the students? Or was it because of my attitude and the things I said? Poor

Frieda! Her hand was cut badly, but she did not want Adrie to see.

I stood up and went to the window. The trees were bare, their limbs like skeletons. The world outside was gray.

This is Berlin, Germany, I thought. *And I do not belong here.*

43
A Gift from My Father

It snowed this week—three days in a row. On Wednesday, after the snow had melted a little and been packed down, I put on my boots and warm jacket and walked to Barret's house. Watcher trotted along ahead of me. Barret had made hot chocolate and cookies. I was always amazed at the things he could do without his sight. Since it was bright and sunny, we brushed off the snow from the picnic table and benches, then sat and enjoyed the bright sunshine. Because it was too slippery to drive, Opa stayed home that day and joined us.

We talked about the terrible fate of the White Rose students. "I wonder if Johanna had to face a guillotine," I said. "I can't bear to think about it."

"Now that you've lived here for a while, how do you feel about your own life here?" Opa asked.

"I don't want to stay here another day."

Opa gave me a long, serious look. "Barret told me you might want a way out."

"I'll go whenever and wherever you say."

"The war is coming closer and will become more violent. It will be more difficult for you to leave by then." He began his usual task of filling his pipe bowl with tobacco. "My advice to you now is to get out while the getting's good—as they say in England."

"But it's winter, Opa," Barret objected. "It would be better to wait until spring, *ja?*"

"By the time she's ready, it will be spring," Opa added. "A few months ago I wouldn't have encouraged your leaving, Wendy, but since the surrender in Stalingrad, and the loss of German submarines in the North Atlantic, I am sure Europe will be invaded before long. Then there will terrible times ahead here in Germany—and Berlin, especially. There is much to do if we are to help you escape. I must contact people along the way who will help you make your way to Denmark."

"Denmark? I never thought of Denmark," I told him.

"Once you are in northern Denmark, you are only a few miles by boat to Sweden, which is neutral and willing to take refugees."

"Is that what I will be? A refugee?"

"*Ja*, you are seeking refuge, right?" Opa answered.

"Oh, Wendy Vendy, I will worry about you . . . ," Barret started to say.

"We must keep personal feelings out of this, Barret," Opa said with a frown. "We will provide Wendy with maps, addresses, names, bus and train routes—along with identification papers." He turned to me. "You will most likely need to show papers at every train depot and border, Wendy. I will get them together for you."

A shiver went up and down my back. Opa spoke rationally and realistically, I knew my escape was really going to happen. But could I do it? Could I get to Denmark by myself in the middle of a war?

"What about money?" I asked. "I don't expect you to provide the funds. I will start saving right away. . . ."

Opa laughed. "Oh, my child, your father prepared for whenever you would need help with your life—either here or in America. He knew quite well, even before you were born, what was ahead here in Germany—especially with Hitler as the Chancellor." Opa motioned to the barn door. "Come in here with me. I have something to show you."

Once inside the barn, Opa opened a cabinet that was stacked with books. He looked them over, then pulled four books from the top shelf. Reaching back into the empty space, he dragged out a rough, unpolished wooden chest. Motioning for us to gather around, he set the chest on the table and turned on the overhead light.

"What is it?" Barret asked.

"A box," I whispered to him.

Opa touched a switch on the box and the cover opened.

I looked inside eagerly, but all it contained was a pile of wooden matches. "Matches?" I asked.

"Matches!" Barret exclaimed.

Opa caught our disappointed expressions and chuckled.

"Just wait." He poured the matches out onto the table. Then, Opa took a small chisel and pried the base of the chest until it popped, revealing a black velvet bag hidden inside.

Opa untied the strong twine that sealed the bag and poured out the contents. A waterfall of precious stones tumbled out, splashing the surface of the table with sparkling colors—emeralds, diamonds, rubies, peridot, yellow citrine—all gleamed like dewdrops and cast little rainbows around the room.

Was I dreaming? I reached out and caught a cobalt-blue sapphire as it rolled across the tabletop. Jewels and gemstones glowed in shades of green, lemon-yellow, pale lilac, and deep purple.

"These are all yours, Wendy," Opa said, "from your father."

I grasped the cold blue jewel tightly in my hand, closed my eyes, and envisioned the blond, smiling man in the photographs.

This treasure was a gift to me from my own father—to protect me. I felt my throat tighten as tears blurred the world around me.

David Dressner, my father whom I never knew—had loved me.

44
Time to Prepare

I sat there staring at the jewels. Neither Opa nor Barret said a word, but Watcher whined and pawed my leg, asking if I was all right.

Finally Opa spoke. "Wendy. Your father suspected the time would come when you would need these jewels. They will enable you to get out of Germany. However, we all know you cannot carry gems like these in your pocket, so we must find a way for you to smuggle them out. While they can be the means for your freedom, they may also be the means for your being robbed, or worse. For now we will keep them here where they have been safe all these years."

Even though we had talked about my leaving Germany, the idea of actually doing it was scary. I had chills as the possibilities of what might happen began to set in.

Opa continued, "Until now, the war has been on the

outskirts of Germany, with bombs concentrating on factories and defense plants. Once the Allies invade Europe, Berlin will be their goal." He gave me a long, serious look. "You must be convinced you're doing the right thing, Wendy. It will not be easy. So, if you are not sure . . ."

"I am sure. I want to leave Germany. When I saw Johanna taken away, and when I heard what they did to the White Rose kids . . ." I nodded. "Yes. I am absolutely sure."

Opa gathered the jewels and put them back in the velvet bag. "Very well. I will begin setting things in motion." Opa put the gems into the box and returned it to its hiding place. "Let's think of way to hide these jewels when you travel."

We were getting warm with our winter jackets still on, so we went outside again. Watcher settled on the snow between Barret and me.

Barret reached down and scratched my dog's head and neck, then paused as his fingers touched Watcher's leather collar. "I know where we can hide the larger jewels."

"Where?" Opa and I asked together.

"We'll hide them in plain sight—on Watcher's jeweled collar!"

"Watcher doesn't have a jeweled collar," I said.

"Not yet," Barret said. "But Heidi did. Opa can replace those fake stones on Heidi's collar with the real jewels." He turned in the direction of his grandfather. "Dogs often have a leather collar with fake jewels fastened to them."

Opa frowned and held his cold pipe in his mouth as he thought about it. After a moment he spoke up. "*Ah, gute*

Idee, Barret. That collar should be a perfect fit for Watcher, now that he's fully grown."

"I'll need to be able to get them off the collar easily," I reminded them.

"*Ja,* of course, Wendy, and we'll keep this in mind," Opa said. "Now I need to get in touch with those who will help you along the way. This may take some time. Letters are in code. Some may be hand delivered on the other end. It may be spring before everything is in place. On the other hand, it may be sooner than we expect. Meanwhile, you should prepare for this journey of yours."

"I'm not sure what I'll need."

"Practical clothing, for one thing. You will need a pair of heavy shoes with thick soles. As you go farther north you may have to walk through bombed-out cities, and there will be broken metal and glass." Opa looked down at my boots. "Those will work well." He nodded.

"Be sure to take a first-aid kit," Barret added.

I glanced at the clock and clamped Watcher's leash onto his present collar. "I must leave. Adrie may be home and wondering where I am and who I've been with." I gave Opa and Barret hugs and headed for the sidewalk.

"Wait! I'll walk a little way with you," Barret called, reaching for his white cane, which he always kept close.

I waited for him and we walked together. "Barret, it seems I must be prepared to leave at any time."

"Opa is eager to get you out of the country before the bombings begin here." Barret paused, as if remembering something. "Wendy, I think he's talked with someone who wants you to leave soon and who is urging him to help."

"Talked with someone? Who?"

Barret shrugged. "I don't know. I have often wondered how he knew you were coming to Berlin when he began the watch on Adrie's house. Have you any idea who it might be?"

"I've wondered the same thing, but I have no idea who it could be."

We stopped at the corner, where we parted ways. Barret took my face in his hands and kissed my cheek. "I wish I could see your pretty face," he said with a sigh.

"You only assume my face is pretty," I told him. "And I will let you believe it."

"I know you are beautiful—inside and out." He kissed my cheek again. "I will miss you when you are gone."

"I will miss you too." I hugged him. *Once I have gone, once the war is over, will I ever see you again?* I wondered. As I clung to Barret I could feel his arms tighten around me. Then he let me go and I headed home.

Waiting

Time now dragged out, and at times it seemed my schemes for escaping Germany were only dreams. Opa was waiting for a message from his contact, and he could not make plans without this person's involvement. "It will happen, Wendy," Opa said. "Be patient."

Spring had come and the grass was turning green and the planes from England were coming closer. The Allies were bombing German airfields and factories. German and American planes fought in the sky and dropped to the Earth in balls of fire. Would I get out of Germany in time?

One night in early May I walked by Adrie's den. She was there listening to BBC—the British Broadcasting Corporation. I could tell she had it on when I heard *da da da BOOM!*—the musical tones from Beethoven's Fifth Symphony. Everyone knew that was the Morse code for the letter *V*—for "Victory." The Allies used that tune all the time, and they held their fingers up in a *V*.

Suddenly a familiar song came from the radio and a well-known voice began to sing.

"That's Drew Winters who is singing!" I exclaimed, rushing into the den. She was about to turn the radio off when I yelled, "Wait! That's my friend Jill's dad!"

"You are not allowed to hear British broadcasting," Adrie stated emphatically.

"But it's Jill's dad. Please, Adrie. It's just a song." I plunked myself on the rug in front of the radio. Drew Winters's beautiful voice floated across the room.

SNAP! Adrie turned the radio off.

I did not want to argue with Adrie, so I went upstairs to my room. I sat on my armchair next to the window and looked out at the dark sky. *I cannot stand one more day here. They watch everything we do; we can't even listen to the music or read the books we want.*

While the following days passed, Watcher and I went on longer walks to build up our strength. I noticed how protective he was of me. Whenever persons came onto our path, Watcher was sure to step around them at a large swath, trying to keep out of their way. I also noted his caution when we passed crowds. Sometimes the fur around his neck bristled if any stranger came too close.

One night when I couldn't sleep, I decided to pack. It was after midnight when I took my backpack out from the closet shelf and put in the things I had listed for the long trek—to Denmark.

After packing I shoved my bag far back on the closet shelf, where it had been since I first arrived. Now I was hungry. I looked at the clock. Two thirty in the morning! Maybe I could sneak downstairs and get something to eat. I tiptoed down the hallway and stairs, went into the kitchen, and turned on the light above the sink. Watcher was asleep on his blanket, and he looked up drowsily when he saw me—his tail thumping.

I was about to close the hall door that led to Frieda's room when I realized her light was still on and her door was open a crack. *Would she like to join me?* I wondered. I treaded silently over the tile floor to her room and rather than startle her, I peeked in first through the crack of the door.

Frieda was sitting at her desk, her back to me. I saw from the reflection in the window by her desk that she was busy writing. It seemed strange she would be up and busy at this late hour.

"Frieda?" I whispered for fear of alarming her. She turned swiftly to me—a look of fear on her face. "It's just me," I said in German. "Would you like some tea?" Frieda and I were conversing more and more often in German.

Relief relaxed her face. "*Ja.* Let's have some tea." She got up from the desk and then motioned to me. "*Komm rein!* Wendy." She gestured me to a chair, and then took both of my hands. "I have something of yours."

She opened a drawer to her desk, fumbled through stationery and papers, and held up a folded paper. "I found it in your shoe the day you were so ill." It was the missing White Rose brochure!

"Oh, Frieda, I wondered what happened to it. I've been so frightened that someone had found it and would tell Adrie."

Frieda's face softened. "*Nein,* darling. I did not feel I had the right to destroy it, but I knew how much trouble you would be in if Adrie found out. So I hid it all this time."

I reached out and hugged her. "I put you in danger too, Frieda. Someone had given the brochure to me because I was curious. I was going to read it and then burn it. When I regained consciousness, I was worried and wondered where it went."

"Do not worry anymore," Frieda said. "Shall we destroy it?"

"*Ja.* Let's burn it now."

Frieda placed the brochure in a dish on her desk, took out a match, and we both watched as the flame slowly danced around the infamous pamphlet. Soon the flames burned brightly. The papers blackened and twisted until they were ashes.

46
Directions for Escape

By July third I was beginning to wonder if the plans we had made would ever happen. I had kept busy all spring, walking, exercising, studying the geography from Berlin to Denmark, and thinking about home in the States. Adrie had gone away last week to somewhere—she would not tell me where—and she did not know when she would be back.

It had been two weeks since I last saw Opa. Since today was Saturday and Opa was usually home on Saturdays, I headed for their house.

"Come in, come in Wendy Vendy," Barret said as he opened the barn door. "Opa was hoping you'd get here today. He's been busy putting things together for you,"

"Come in, my child," Opa called. "*Ja,* everything is ready for you to leave soon, but there is much for me to explain to you."

Watcher and I went to the worktable, where a large silk map of Europe was spread. Opa traced his finger along a red line he had drawn. "Here is Berlin," he said. "There is a train system to Hamburg from here. You will need these identity papers on the train and other places, if necessary." He handed me two copies of cleverly forged German birth certificates.

"The name on here is Karin Nelson," I said curiously.

"That's your new name, Wendy—from the moment you get on the train," Barret said. "Otherwise Adrie or her people will be able to trace you."

"Remember, while you are in Germany, you are a German citizen." Opa handed me an official-looking Swedish document with a gold seal. It also had the name, Karin Nelson. "When you get to Denmark, you will still be German, since Denmark is occupied by Germany. However, in Sweden, you will use this birth certificate. You are then a Swedish citizen. This Swedish document was the most difficult to get. We hope by then the Red Cross will have this name listed and they will be expecting you. We do not want to use your American birth certificate or your real name. You must never use your name Wendy Dekker or your American name, Wendy Taylor, when you leave your house for the last time."

"Will my mom and dad in America know I'm going by the name Karin Nelson?"

"Yes, they know everything. So again, use only the name Karin Nelson once you leave. A slip of the tongue and you can be sure you will be found out. However, Adrie will be unable to trace Karin Nelson, a Swedish girl."

"I don't speak Swedish."

"You speak German, and that will be enough. If anyone asks, why you are in Denmark, explain you were visiting Germany and you need to get back to Sweden."

Each birth certificate had a photograph of me. "Where did you get the picture?" I asked.

"I took it one day at the park with this." Opa pulled a pen from his shirt pocket. "No one suspects you are taking a picture. I have more things you will need," Opa continued, showing me a small can of beef—or so the label said. He demonstrated a secret way of opening the can. "The silk map folds easily to hide inside."

Then he displayed a jackknife and popped open the blade. "This is for you to keep in your rucksack along with the false can of beef. The blade is very strong. You'll want it to pry things open, or to remove the stones from Watcher's collar as you need them."

He handed me the jackknife, and I discovered it also hid a screwdriver, a can opener, and a little fork/spoon.

Barret felt with his hand across the table and retrieved a leather harness. "Here is Heidi's old work harness. Watcher did well with it when we practiced with him. Take it home now, but hide it."

"Dogs may not be allowed on the train or boats, but a seeing-eye dog will be given permission to go with you. You will pretend to be blind, won't you?" Opa asked.

"Yes," I answered. "It will help me in many situations, I'm sure."

Opa asked me at our last meeting to bring him my hiking boots. Now he placed them on the table, turned them over, and showed me how each heel opened into a hollow space. He reached inside and pulled out money. "In your right shoe I have inserted German Reichs marks and Swedish money—along with several of the smaller gemstones. You can sell them to a jeweler if you need money." He opened the heel in the left shoe, drew out a folded sheet of paper, and handed it to me. "You must keep this list of names and addresses well hidden. If anyone should find it, many lives would be in danger."

"I'll guard it with my very life," I promised.

Opa pointed to the first name. "When you arrive in Hamburg, this is where you will go. You must say, 'I am looking for my father, Herr Nelson. Is he here?' He will answer with, 'He went back to Sweden. I am Otto. Come in.' Now you will know you are in the right place. He is an old friend who lives in Hamburg with his sister. His last name is not here in order to protect them. Give him this blue sapphire." He pointed to a deep blue stone on Watcher's collar. "For this stone Otto will see that you get to passage into Copenhagen, Denmark." I watched as Opa's finger traced the map to Copenhagen, the capital of Denmark. "Most likely Otto will send you to Denmark by ship. If so, you will give the captain a stone—perhaps this blue garnet—for the risk he is taking by transporting you in his boat." He handed me the stone.

"A blue garnet?" I asked. "I thought garnets were red."

"A blue garnet is rare, and although it is small, it is valuable. Otto will know its value." He touched a square red gem. "This is another treasure—a red emerald. The unusual colors of the stones enhance their value."

"The jewels are so beautiful; I hate to part with them." I pointed to a pale green stone.

"What is this? It's too light to be an emerald."

Opa picked up the stone and put it in my hand. "This peridot came from the sky. It was found in a meteorite." Opa smiled as he remembered. "David said to tell you he would give you the stars if he could."

"Oh, it came from the stars! I will keep this one for myself forever."

Opa smiled. "Yes, he loved you, my child. Now, let's get back to your trip."

I took a deep breath. "I hope I can remember everything."

"Once you are in Copenhagen, you must contact this couple," Opa continued, indicating the address on the list. "Pier and Ingrid are jewelers who knew your father, David. Their jewelry store is Solstice Jewelry. They are very happy to help you—for David's sake. Use the same code, asking for Herr Nelson. Their answer will be 'He went back to Sweden.' You will give them this pigeon-blood ruby." He tapped his finger on the darkest red stone on Watcher's collar. "They have arranged for another fishing boat to take you to Sweden. You might give that captain this large fire opal."

He folded the list carefully and replaced it in the heel of my boot.

"Remember, Wendy, guard this list," Opa warned again. "Do not let anyone get it under any circumstances. These friends take money or jewels so they can continue to help Jews and other prisoners get away. They are risking their own lives when they help someone to escape, and at some point they may need to flee themselves."

"I understand, Opa." I snapped my fingers. "Come here, Watcher. Let's try on your work harness." My dog came and sat at my feet patiently while I put the work harness on him.

Opa took a satchel from the table and placed the jeweled collar inside. "Don't set that bag down anywhere on the way home," Opa warned. "The gems are valued at thousands of dollars."

"I'll guard it carefully," I promised, tapping the sack. "This is my ticket to freedom."

"Which reminds me," Opa said, handing me another envelope. "Your ticket to Hamburg."

I opened the envelope. The ticket was stamped *Monday, July 5, 1943, 6 a.m.* "That's the day after tomorrow!"

47
Good-Bye to Frieda and Adrie

I put everything in a bag to carry home, headed to the door, and then remembered something. "Opa," I said, turning back, "you were watching Adrie's house, knowing I would be coming to Germany—to Berlin. So many times I've wondered how you knew."

Opa smiled. "I didn't know you well enough at first to confide that information to you for fear you might tell Adrie. Since you haven't asked since then, I haven't brought it up."

"Will you tell me now? How did you know I was on my way to Germany?"

"It was Nixie—your mother in America—who contacted me."

I felt a rush of love. "How did she know you?"

"Have you forgotten that both Adrie and Nixie were born in Germany? When Nixie went to study in America, she chose to become a citizen. I met Nixie several times when she visited Adrie here in Berlin. She stayed in touch with me over the years and sent me photographs of you from the time you were born. That is how I recognized you when I saw you. I gave those photos to your father, David."

"So when she heard Adrie and I disappeared from Maine, she was sure we'd go to Germany?"

"Oh, *Ja*. She begged me to care for you if you needed help. I promised her I would. We have been able to communicate several times—secretly, of course."

"Does she know I want to leave Germany?"

"Your parents are working to make arrangements for you once you get to Sweden." Opa reached out and clasped both of my hands in his. "Wendy, you know how much they love you. You were their little girl too."

"Oh, yes, yes. I do know." My eyes filled with tears as I kissed Opa. "Thank you for all the kindness and caring you've shown to me. Thank you for being my grandfather. I will never forget you." As I turned away, I saw tears in Opa's eyes too.

Barret walked with Watcher and me as I headed back to Lindenstrasse. We were quiet for a while. My heart raced as I thought about the trip and danger ahead, but Barret must have known my feelings, as he held my hand firmly. We stopped when we reached the park, and he let go of my hand.

"I will miss you terribly, Barret." My voice shook. "But it is time for me to leave . . . to go home—to America."

Barret reached out to me, kissed me first on the cheek, and then sweetly on the lips. "Good-bye, my Wendy

Vendy," he whispered. "God be with you." He held me tightly for a few moments, then turned and walked swiftly away, his white cane clicking on the sidewalk.

When I got home, I went to my room and hid everything Opa had given me under my bed until I could pack it. Then I joined Frieda in the kitchen. Watcher was under the table, gobbling up his supper, and I realized with a start that I had not removed his work harness.

"Come here, Watcher," I said. He came to me, although he eyed his dish as if to say, *I haven't finished yet.*

"That's a different harness, isn't it?" Frieda asked.

"*Ja.* It's so I can teach him how to be a guide dog—in case I ever need a guide dog." I grinned at her as I unhitched the harness.

Frieda did not ask how I got it, but she gave me a curious look as she filled my plate with a delicious *süss-saure Klopse*—sweet-and-sour meatballs—on boiled potatoes. We ate dinner quietly, and I had an uncomfortable feeling that she sensed something was up.

After supper I ran upstairs. I had lots to think about before my trip. My knapsack was already packed and on the floor of my closet.

I was about to pack away the secret things Opa had given me today when suddenly I stopped, realizing that I hadn't put my knapsack on the floor of my closet. I had set it on the top shelf. I was certain of that. So how did it get on the floor? Perhaps it had fallen down while I was gone.

I picked it up and looked inside. Everything seemed to be in order—except there was a small leather pouch that I did not recognize. Puzzled, I took it out and opened it. Inside was a wad of Germany money. Where had it come from? Had Frieda put it in there? She was the only person who had been home today. If she had looked in my backpack, she would know I was preparing to leave. I wasn't sure if I should ask her, but who else could it be?

I went down to the kitchen where Frieda was cleaning up the last bit of dishes. "Is this yours?" I asked, holding up the leather pouch.

She didn't answer right away and then she sat at the table. "It is yours now, Wendy."

"There is a lot of money here. Why did you put it in my rucksack?"

"I want you to have it. You will need it if . . ." Frieda took a deep breath. "Let me explain. Your rucksack fell today as I was cleaning." She looked down at her clasped hands. "It was not zipped up, and things fell out. I realized that you might be planning to go away. I may be wrong, and if so, forgive me, but it is easy to see you are not happy in Germany. I saw your reaction to the execution of the White Rose students—and your deep sadness for your friend Johanna." She paused and scrutinized me expectantly. When I said nothing, she went on. "I assume you've decided to leave—perhaps to a neutral country. If it were possible, I would go away with you, but since I cannot, I want to help you escape if you can. The money is what I have saved over the years. You must get away before the war escalates even more."

I went to Frieda and hugged her. "Oh, Frieda, come with me. We'll go together."

"Oh, my darling child, I can't. I am too old for a venture like yours. Besides, Adrie trusts me and now she will be alone. I can at least stay and help her to get through whatever is ahead. If there is a God in Heaven, He must do something to stop this evil war."

"You have been so quiet about—everything. When I saw how you cut your hand, I knew you were unhappy with what happened to the White Rose students."

"I could not speak of my feelings to Adrie—or to you until now. Your mother put all her hope in the Führer and the Third Reich. When Germany is defeated, and it will be defeated, all Adrie's false dreams will end. Pity her, Wendy. She is a lost soul—and now she is about to lose you."

"I can never forgive or forget what happened to Johanna and the Bible Students, or to the Jews, the White Rose students, or those babies in the Lebensborn," I admitted. "Perhaps someday I will be able at least to pity Adrie and the others who allowed the unforgivable to happen." I put my arms around Frieda. "I will never forget you, Frieda, and the sweet love and kindness you've shown me."

Sunday night I sat at my desk and pulled out a box of stationery that Adrie had given to me and wrote the following letter.

Dear Adrie:

I am not happy to leave you. I remember all the wonderful, sweet things you have done for me all *my life. I have left because I cannot live in Nazi Germany. I am not a German girl. I am an American girl.*

I must go away to a place where I can have freedom to question or protest, to speak up, to be brave.

I know you wanted the best for me. However, I cannot be what I am not. Inside I am and will always be Wendy Taylor from America.

I love you.

Wendy

PS I am leaving your ruby ring. I do not feel I deserve to have it, because I am not the wonderful German daughter you want me to be. I am also leaving the three wise monkeys because they are not wise. They are blind and deaf and mute about the evil in the world.

I placed the letter on the top of my desk—along with Adrie's ruby ring and the bracelet.

48
Runaways

It was almost three thirty in the morning and the first faint light of dawn crept over the eastern sky. I strapped the work harness, along with his precious collar, onto Watcher. After I hitched him to his guide dog harness, he ran to the bedroom door and scratched at it, his tail wagging wildly in anticipation of a walk.

"No, no, Watcher. Quiet!" I said in English.

Watcher, who now understood commands in German and English, looked disappointed. However, he obeyed, lay flat on the floor, and watched me expectantly while I dressed into my traveling clothes—a plain brown skirt and a white shirt. I added a tan jacket, as it might be cold at this time of the morning, even in July. I also wore the strong boots to protect my feet—and to protect the precious secrets inside them. I would not be fashionable, but I would be inconspicuous.

After sliding my arms into my rucksack and adjusting the weight onto my shoulders, I went downstairs with Watcher at my heels.

The house was silent—no sign of Frieda. I looked around at the beautiful residence, so tastefully decorated by Adrie's artistic hand. "Good-bye, house," I whispered.

We slipped out the door and headed toward the bus stop. After midnight the bus came every hour until six o'clock in the morning. I began my blind act even though it was still dark, and put on my sunglasses. This way no one could see my eyes, in case I unconsciously gazed in the direction of movements or sights. It was four o'clock when the bus arrived. Watcher did exactly as he should, pausing as the door opened and then climbing in with me.

"Good dog," the driver said admiringly. I paid the fare I had set aside in the pocket of my jacket. "Where are you going, *Fräulein*?"

"To *zum Bahnof*."

"I will call it out when we arrive," he promised.

"Danke." Evidently my disguise was working.

I glanced discreetly at my ticket when I arrived at the train terminal. Track four was where my train to Hamburg was waiting. I purchased a cup of coffee and a slice of coffee cake from a vendor, and paid with the correct change, the way I had seen Barret tell the size of coins by fingering them. The server put the items in a bag and tapped my arm. "Here is your purchase."

"Danke," I said, and sat down on a nearby bench.

I gave Watcher a doggy bone from my rucksack. "That's all you can eat until we get to Hamburg," I told him. He devoured the bone eagerly, then sat up and looked around.

As I ate my coffee cake, I noticed the waiting room was filling up with early travelers. A few people looked at us curiously. I pretended not to notice. Suddenly Watcher began to wiggle and his tail pounded on the tile floor. He whined, then barked and stood up.

"What is it, Watcher?" I asked softly. "Come. Sit."

He looked at me quizzically, whined again, and then he pulled away before I could grab his harness. Watcher bounded across the huge waiting room to a familiar figure, circled him several times, and then lay on the floor in front of him, quivering. I lifted up my dark glasses to see better, and gasped.

It was Barret! Had he come to say good-bye? Did he have a message for me?

"Barret!" I hurried across the busy waiting area. Barret appeared to be hesitant and uncertain as he stood there.

"Here I am, Barret." As I linked my arm in his, I noticed he had a large backpack. "Why are you here? Where are you going?"

"With you," he said. "I've decided to leave Berlin with you."

My heart almost jumped out of my chest with joy and relief. "Oh, Barret, I'm so happy you decided to come! I can't believe you changed your mind!" I paused, and then added, "I hope I didn't talk you into something you'll regret."

"You didn't talk me into it, Wendy. I made my own decision. I had never really discussed it with Opa, but after you left, we talked about my leaving. Berlin will be a major target soon, and Opa agreed I would be safer somewhere else. He went right to work and was able to get my papers ready—using the same papers and contacts as yours—all except the Swedish birth certificate. There wasn't enough time to get one. But hopefully it won't cause a problem."

"But what about Opa? He'll be all alone."

"That's another thing. Opa says he will be investigated soon. There is a rift in his organization. Hitler has evidence that there is a traitor somewhere in that group. I am worried that something Opa did in the past may be exposed. Opa insisted I must leave, or I might be caught up in the problem and be ostracized too." Barret closed his eyes, and I saw a tear slip out from under his lashes. "It was hard to leave. However, the thought of leaving with you made it easier."

I put my hand on his arm. "I am so happy that you are coming. I hope Opa will be safe."

"I hope so too. I fear for him." Barret opened his wristwatch and felt the hands. "It's time to board. We better get to our train."

No one questioned our identity when we showed our papers and tickets at Track four. The conductor, noticing Watcher was a guide dog, motioned us on board.

Once we settled in our seats with Watcher curled up at

our feet, Barret reached out his hand. "Allow me to introduce myself. I am Conrad Nelson, your brother."

"And I am Karin Nelson, your sister," I said, shaking his hand.

It was still hard to believe that Barret was actually with me, as I had made up my mind I would be going without him. But there he was, sitting beside me and holding on to my hand.

"Opa is relieved I will be out of Berlin." Barret leaned closer and whispered, "However, he knows of particular danger ahead in Hamburg, and he wants us to go immediately to Denmark."

"What danger?"

Barret put his finger to his lips. "I will tell you when we get to Hamburg."

49
Hiding in Hamburg

I slept most of the way to Hamburg with my head resting on Barret's shoulder, except for the times I took Watcher out for a walk at various stops. Security was strict; at each stop, Barret and I had to show our papers.

I could see where bombs had destroyed areas of towns that had been undamaged when I'd traveled through them a year ago. *Allied planes are coming closer,* Opa had said.

"We will soon be there," Barret whispered as we approached Hamburg. "We need to get in touch with our contact."

I sat up and removed the list of names from the hiding place in the heel of my boot. "The name is Otto, and the address is listed. Shall we call him first?"

"*Nein.* Phone calls can be traced. Let's find a place to eat. Then we'll get a taxi."

Outside the station, we found a nearby restaurant.

After a discussion with a waiter about letting Watcher come in with us, he led us to a table in the rear of the dining room.

While we waited for our food, I whispered to Barret, "What was Opa's warning? You said you'd tell me when we reached Hamburg."

Barret leaned closer and covered his mouth with his hand. "Opa says Hamburg will be bombed by American and British planes any day now. It will be a disaster—not a few planes, but hundreds." Barret paused, took a sip of coffee, and sat closer to me. "The Allies call it Operation Gomorrah."

"That name Gomorrah means complete destruction, doesn't it?" I asked. "I can't help but wonder how Opa gets all this information. And that he tells you everything, Barret."

"*Ja.* He has his secret sources and he trusts me. He worries about me . . . with my . . . disability . . . that I need to be aware of what is going on, especially if anything happens to him."

"But it also puts you in a dangerous position. What else did he tell you—about Hamburg?"

"The first planes will drop silver foil that will make German radar useless. It is something new that the Allies are trying. We have to get out of Hamburg before that takes place. Opa says once the actual bombing starts, there will be total destruction."

"When will this take place?"

"Very soon. We must get to Denmark quickly."

When we went out to the street, we were shocked to hear terrified voices of people running and pointing to the sky. Watcher barked, and leaped at thousands of leaflets that fell from a plane that circled the city. White packets dropped onto the streets, sidewalks, and cars.

"What's happening?" Barret asked.

"We're being bombed with some kind of leaflets." The screams and shrieks of pedestrians mixed with the wails of air-raid sirens. I looked up, but the plane had disappeared into the clouds.

I reached down and picked up a leaflet. "It's not foil. Just paper." Relieved, I read the title: "'The Manifesto of the Students of Munich.' Barret, it's the sixth letter from the White Rose group! The whole city is bombarded with copies of it!" I wanted to cheer. Even though the student leaders had been executed and the rest were in jail, somehow their work went on and more people than ever were reading their message. I was relieved to see the plane had disappeared before Nazi planes went after it.

The taxi ride to our first contact seemed long. Eventually the cab pulled up to a sidewalk and a row of apartment houses. "I hope you kids have money to pay for this trip," the taxi driver said as he pulled our backpacks out from the trunk.

"Our grandfather gave us a little spending money," Barret said as he got out of the taxi with Watcher.

"*Danke,*" I said, handing the driver the exact amount along with a small tip. Already Frieda's purse had helped us on our journey. The driver would be shocked if he knew the treasure in jewels we had with us.

We went inside to the vestibule of the apartment house. We did not know the last name of our contact—only the apartment number: 301. I pushed the button for apartment 301.

"Who is there?" asked a man's voice.

"I am looking for my father, Herr Nelson. Is he here?"

"He went back to Sweden. I am Otto. Come in." The buzzer went off, and I held the door open for Barret and Watcher.

"It worked!" I whispered.

We walked up three flights of stairs to Otto's apartment. A middle-aged man with a beard and mustache stood in a doorway, waiting. "I am Otto," he said, motioning for us to come in.

A short, round woman, with white braids encircling her head peeked out from the kitchen. "*Willkommen!* I am Ulla, Otto's sister,"

"How do you do?" Barret said. "I am Conrad Nelson, and this is my sister, Karin."

Ulla came slowly into the hallway, her eyes on Watcher. "Does the dog bite?"

"Not unless we tell him to," Barret answered.

"Actually, he's a sweet dog," I added quickly.

Otto led us into living room. "Sit down, children. We have much to discuss. I am waiting to hear from a fisherman who will take you by boat to Copenhagen. However, it will have to be under secret and dangerous circumstances. Dangerous because the German navy is patrolling all the waters around Copenhagen and often stops boats to investigate the ships. They will immediately arrest Jews, as well as those they think might be members of the Resistance."

"We are not Jews, and we do have papers to prove we are German citizens," Barret offered. "Perhaps we should go by train?"

"It will be equally dangerous," Otto said. "All border crossings into Denmark are under strict surveillance."

I was sure Otto and Ulla noticed the disappointment on our faces because Ulla spoke up quickly. "You are welcome to stay here with us until Otto makes contact with the captain. You will be safe here. Did anyone see you as you came up the stairs? Anyone in the apartments below?"

"I didn't see anyone," I said.

"How long do you think it will be before you hear?" Barret asked.

"Only a day or two."

"No sooner? We must to get out of Hamburg soon . . . in case it is bombed." Barret chose his words carefully.

"Oh, Hamburg is safe. The city is encircled with antiaircraft defense stations, and now we have complete radar protection. It's safer here than anywhere."

"Oh, *Ja*," Ulla added. "The radar can tell us in advance if bombers are coming from a hundred miles or more. And there are about two thousand shelters."

"*Ach!* You will be out on the sea before Hamburg is bombed," Otto assured us. "You'll be fine here for now."

"What do you think, Conrad?" I asked Barret.

"It's the only thing we can do."

Later, when we were alone, I whispered to Barret, "Should we tell these people about the coming bombing? After all, they are risking their own lives to save us."

"When we are safely on board the ship," Barret answered.

For the next few days we stayed in Otto's apartment. I slept on a cot in Ulla's room while Barret slept on a couch. Watcher slept in the kitchen, where Ulla fed him scraps, and lost her fear of my big dog.

Every morning Otto went into Hamburg to meet with his "sources." One day he came home much earlier than usual. We heard his footsteps running up the stairs and then he burst into the apartment. "The Gestapo is going house-to-house in this area, searching for members of the Resistance." He peered out the window. "They are on this street now! Thank the good Lord I made it back here in time," he said breathlessly. "They will be here soon. We could try to bluff them—I could say you are my niece and nephew. However, I am concerned they will be suspicious, even with the guide dog. They'd take you away for questioning." He turned to me. "I am wondering if your mother—Adrie—might have a search out for you, Karin. Opa told me that your mother has connections with the *Abwehr*. She knows you took your dog. So I prefer that you all hide."

He rushed us into his bedroom and opened a closet door. He reached behind the clothing that hung inside, turned a latch, and a section of the back wall opened. "Get in, get in! *Schnell!*"

I took Barret's hand and pulled him through the clothing and into the dark recess of the hiding place. "Come, Watcher!" I whispered, and my dog followed. We could hear banging on the doors below. Watcher began to whine. His ear perked up and he let out a yelp.

"They're here. Don't let him bark," Otto warned. "Keep him quiet."

"Hide!" I commanded my dog. Immediately he stretched out onto the rough floor of the secret place and put his head on his front legs.

Otto closed the hidden door and left us in complete darkness. Barret and I clung to each other, and I burrowed my face in his chest to drown out the sounds of my fast breathing.

I could hear Otto straighten out the clothing that hung in the closet and then quietly close the closet door.

Within moments there was more loud banging and men's forceful voices. The sound of heavy boots echoed, and I felt myself trembling. The Gestapo were in the bedroom! The closet door had opened. If we were found hiding, we would certainly be considered guilty and arrested.

We didn't breathe. We didn't move. Watcher obeyed my "hide" command, and remained silent. I could tell the police were shoving aside the clothing on the closet racks. Then the outer door slammed and the footsteps faded. I realized how protected I had been when living with Adrie. Now I was nobody—and could be questioned or treated cruelly, like anyone else. Even more reason for us to get away from Germany soon.

50
Inferno!

Later that evening Otto told us, "I've arranged for you to leave tomorrow on a fishing trawler. This captain is willing to take you to Copenhagen, since you have German papers. However, officers on German ships search private boats, so you must be prepared to answer questions in the event that this happens. German ships patrol the waters around the Baltic Sea and Copenhagen regularly."

"Just take us to the boat and we'll be on our way," Barret said.

"*Gut!* Be ready to leave early in the morning."

Dawn was slowly lighting up the eastern sky when we climbed into Otto's car and headed out. We were far beyond the outskirts of Hamburg when we heard the sound of air-raid sirens. My heart sank.

Otto pulled over to the side of the road. "I have no idea

if there are shelters nearby. But we are so far out of the city, we should be all right. The U-boat pens, the ports, and the industrial section of Hamburg are the likely targets." Otto thought for a moment, and then said, "There's a shortcut to the little fishing village where your boat is waiting. It is a dirt road most of the way, but it is more direct to the dock where the boat is hidden."

I peered through the window to the overhead sky. "They're dropping something—glittery things."

"It's the foil," Barret exclaimed. "They're blocking German radar. The bombers are on their way. There will be hundreds of planes! We've got to get out of here before the bombs start falling."

"How far away is the boat?" I asked Otto.

Otto stepped on the gas and we turned down a hard-packed, bumpy dirt road. "We'll be there soon."

After a while, we heard the thunder of planes that now darkened the sky. Bombs began to drop like eagles diving for their prey. We could see sudden bursts of flames rising from the direction of the city.

"They're dropping fire bombs, too!" I cried out.

"These are only the first group," Barret said.

As we approached an open area near the shore, I could see part of the Hamburg skyline. Flames had quickly shot up hundreds of feet into the air. "The wind is building up from the fires and tossing sparks and embers everywhere," I exclaimed. "I can see trees and houses—buildings—everything is burning. The fire is spreading like a tornado all over Hamburg!"

"Keep heading along the water, Otto," Barret called. "Hurry."

We were soon in a wooded area where trees blocked the view of the city. Yet the whole sky was brilliant from the fires. After several miles, we drove through a small village.

"The fishing boat is concealed down the footpath in a cove." Otto pointed to a dark path almost hidden from sight. "Get your things, and I'll take you to the boat."

We walked for a mile or so through the overgrown trail. Otto led the way, and I followed him. Barret held on to my backpack, and Watcher raced back and forth around us.

"The cove is just ahead," Otto finally said. "There!"

We turned into the cove, where an old fishing boat was tied to a rickety dock. I stopped and asked, "Is this the boat? It is old! Is it safe?" I could not hide the dismay in my voice.

"It's old but serviceable with a fairly new diesel engine," Otto replied. "It's registered as German, so there should be no problem in Denmark."

I must have looked worried, because Otto went on to assure me. "Karin, it's a seaworthy ship. I have known Captain Lichtenberg for years. He'll take good care of you."

Otto helped Barret climb on board, and Watcher leaped in after him. I tossed my knapsack onto the deck and then I hopped on too.

"Josef?" Otto yelled. "Are you here, Josef?"

"I'm here!" a hearty voice called out, and a tall, rugged man appeared from the cabin. A younger man came up behind him.

Otto introduced us to Captain Lichtenberg, who shook hands with us—including Watcher, who held out his paw.

Peder Fischer, the captain's first mate, introduced himself and laughed. "Peder Fischer—a perfect name for a fisherman."

The captain put his arm around Otto's shoulders. "We don't say '*Sieg Heil*' around here anymore. We say, 'Survive, my friend.' He gestured to the black clouds of smoke over Hamburg. "This attack looks bad."

"*Ja*—so get these young people safely to Copenhagen soon."

"I will," Captain Lichtenberg promised, and then turned to us. "Welcome aboard."

"Is it safe for us to leave now, with bombers coming?" I asked nervously.

"I don't think they'll target us—we're small and insignificant," Captain Lichtenberg answered. "The reason for the fires is to light up Hamburg for the next group of bombers—American planes. Hopefully, they won't pay attention to one little boat on the sea."

"Before we leave, I have something for you, Otto." Reaching into my deep pocket, I pulled out the sapphire I had hidden, and dropped it into his hand. "Thank you for all you've done for us. And thank Ulla, too. I pray she is safe."

"I must get back right away." Before leaving, Otto gave us a mock salute as he climbed onto the wharf. "Safe journey, children! I'll let Opa know your progress."

Peder was now unhitching the ropes that tied the boat

to the dock as Captain Lichtenberg started up the engine.

"How long will it take to get to Copenhagen?" Barret asked over the sound.

"It all depends on how far off course I must go to keep away from German patrol boats. I know their schedules pretty well, but one never knows, especially now, with this bombing on Hamburg. We have nothing to hide, but it would be better not to be questioned."

"If a naval ship should stop us, you have the proper papers," Peder said. "But you, Karin, don't talk too much. You have an American accent they might catch."

As we moved slowly out of the cove and headed to sea, I watched the distant fires and the pillars of smoke that reached into the sky. I could see the black columns twist into tornadoes that carried embers and scattered sparks, igniting even more fires.

The planes were gone. "The next group will be coming soon to bomb," the captain predicted. "If there's anything left to bomb, that is."

Before long, the city of Hamburg was only a glow against the skyline. The salty sea, the waves, and the bitter smell of diesel fumes finally overpowered the blowing smoke of the inferno.

51
Threats

Far out on the ocean the wind was strong and the waves sprayed mist over the bow. It was restful to be away from the war and bombs, although I knew ships and submarines of many nations prowled these waters.

"I hope you don't get seasick, Karin," Peder said in a teasing tone.

"After being torpedoed in a U-boat under the sea—this is nothing," I bragged. "Have you ever been torpedoed—or under the sea in a submarine?"

"*Nein*—you are a true heroine, Karin. You deserve the Iron Cross." He winked at the captain, who laughed, and I felt a flash of annoyance.

Barret and Watcher were huddled together on the floor underneath an old canvas tarp. I pushed myself in with them and realized they were both asleep, although Watcher woke up and moved over for me. The canvas smelled of oil and fish, but it kept out the wind, and after I settled next to Barret, I was soon asleep too.

The drone of the engine that lulled me to sleep stopped, and I awoke. As I peeked out from under the tarp, I saw a patrol boat had pulled up and two naval officers were climbing aboard.

What if they suspect we are runaways escaping Germany? What if Adrie sent them after me? I ducked back under the tarp, hoping I hadn't been seen.

One of the naval officers came over and yanked the canvas from the three of us. For a moment he stood there—tall, cold, and solemn.

"Get up!" he ordered. "Give me your papers."

When Barret and I stood up, Watcher did also. I heard a low growl coming from his throat, and the fur on his back stood up. Seldom did Watcher growl at anyone. The officer frowned at my dog, and I could see him fingering the revolver on his belt.

"Hush, Watcher," I whispered.

Watcher looked up at me and then sat next to my feet.

I dug into my backpack and handed the officer the German birth certificate and ID that Opa had made for me.

"Karin Nelson?"

"*Ja.*"

"Why are you going to Copenhagen?"

"I am going to Copenhagen to study . . . Norse history."

"And you couldn't do that in Berlin?"

"Not as well as in Denmark."

"You have a strange accent. You are German?"

"Ja." I had to think quickly. "I had a difficult throat surgery this past spring, and . . . er . . . my voice and diction were affected. Here, I have documentation if you want to see it."

He did not answer; instead he rudely shoved his hand out to me.

I showed him the health certificate Opa suggested I should bring. It recorded my quinsy throat surgery. Fortunately, the health certificate did not use my name, but only the term *This Patient.*

Apparently, it satisfied the officer's needs because he shoved the papers back at me and then turned to Barret. "You have papers? You are blind, are you? Can you find them for me?"

"I'll get them for you, Conrad," I offered.

"*Nein!* I asked him," the officer snapped.

"It's all right, Karin," Barret said, a warning in his voice. He stooped down and reached for his rucksack, opened the front pocket, and pulled out the papers Opa had made. He was about to hand them to the officer when a series of large waves rocked the boat, and Barret lost his balance. As he fell, the papers scattered over the deck.

I reached to help him up, but the officer shoved me out of the way. "Let him get up himself. Who are you, his keeper?"

"I'm his sister," I said angrily. "And you are not a gentleman!"

Instantly he slapped my face so hard, it knocked me

to the deck. "Do not talk back to a German officer."

In a flash Watcher leaped at the man, his teeth bared.

"No, Watcher!" I yelled. "Come here!"

My dog stopped his attack and came quickly to my side. "Sit!" Watcher sat close to me, but his eyes were on the man who had slapped me. My face smarted, and my knees were bleeding from the contact with the rough deck.

Captain Lichtenberg put his hands up in a calming gesture, and whispered something to the other officer who was questioning him. Evidently, this officer was of a higher rank, and he shouted to the bully, "My, you are a brave one, aren't you, Lieutenant? Picking on a blind boy and a pretty young girl?" He pointed at us. "Help them up and apologize! These are German citizens, not criminals. And the girl is right—you are not a gentleman."

The lieutenant's face reddened with anger. He grabbed my arm, but I pulled away and brushed my sleeve, as if it were polluted from his touch. When I stood up, we faced each other for a few moments, and I could see retaliation in his eyes. "I will be watching for you when you arrive in Copenhagen," he whispered.

Barret was able to gather his papers, and he stood with them in his hand. The lieutenant grabbed them, looked them over, and then handed them back.

"Everything is in order," the superior officer announced. "We won't detain you any longer." He turned to me. "Please forgive my impulsive companion here. I will see he is reprimanded for his insolence." The men climbed back aboard their ship. The engine started, and I could see the lieutenant still glaring at me as they backed away.

"Will they be in Copenhagen?" I asked our captain. "That lieutenant threatened me."

"It may be their home base. I hope not. He did not like you, Karin. Keep in mind that you must not speak back to any Nazi officers. They are arrogant and enjoy being cruel. You just have to let them have their imagined superiority—and then laugh at them when they're gone."

"The other officer took my side," I pointed out. "He was kind."

"Ah, I think that captain was smitten by your beautiful face," Peder teased.

I felt my cheeks burn, but it was nice to have a compliment for a change.

52
Trouble in Copenhagen

The next afternoon, when we pulled into a Copenhagen port authority, I was dismayed to see the same German patrol ship docked nearby.

"Let me have your papers," Captain Lichtenberg whispered. "We'll get this over with quickly."

We gathered our things and then followed the captain and Peder up the wharf to the customs and immigration office.

Captain Lichtenberg did not appear worried, and he spoke to the authorities, introduced us as his passengers, and showed his papers and ours. A woman at the desk looked everything over, and stamped some of the documents. Then she noticed Watcher.

"Is that a guide dog?" she asked in German. I noticed a wooden plaque on her desk with the name Inga Josephson.

Barret answered. "I am blind and this is my dog."

"Just a moment, please." She disappeared into another office and closed the door.

"What's happening?" I whispered to Captain Lichtenberg.

He shrugged.

When the door opened again, Inga Josephson came out—along with the lieutenant who had threatened me. "The officer here warned me about that dog," she said. "He's been waiting around, knowing you'd be arriving soon. He says that animal must not be allowed into the country."

"What do you mean? He warned you about our dog?" I felt anger mounting.

"He said the dog attacked him when he boarded your boat."

"Not true!" Captain Lichtenberg bellowed. "This officer attacked the girl. The dog was protecting her."

"Show us your wounds—the bite marks," Peder demanded of the lieutenant. "Show us!"

"I will only show my bruises to my doctor and my lawyer!"

"He's lying," I said. "He threatened me! He said he'd get even with me when we got to Copenhagen."

Inga looked from the Lieutenant to the captain, back to me, then to Barret. "I'm sorry," she said. "I don't know whom to believe. There is only one thing to do until I get a police officer or judge—or someone in authority here. We have a kennel to hold animals that enter the country under quarantine. Once they are pronounced healthy, their owners can retrieve them. We'll simply put your dog there until we can establish if he is dangerous." Once again she left us and went down a hallway to another office.

The lieutenant, who had been standing by, sneered at me. "I'll have that dog destroyed tomorrow. That will teach you never to ridicule or embarrass a German officer!"

The woman came back up the hall with a man in work clothes. "Give me the dog. I'll put him in the kennel," he said in German.

My voice was rising. "No! This . . . person . . . says he will have him destroyed."

"Nein," the worker said. "I will not let that happen."

Barret reached out for me and pulled me close to him. "Let them have him," he whispered. "We'll come back later. But take the collar off."

I had forgotten about the collar. Watcher was more important to me than the jewels, but I knew we could not survive what might be ahead without them.

"I'll take his collar and his harness," I said reluctantly. "We will be back, you can be sure of that." I turned to the lieutenant. "And if you lay a hand on him . . ." I was shouting now. "If you lay a hand on him, I will have Adolf Hitler himself destroy you!"

The lieutenant burst out laughing. "Oh, I'm shaking in fear."

"You should believe her," Captain Lichtenberg said. "She comes from powerful people."

I had no idea why the captain said that, but I was glad

he did. Perhaps it might worry the cruel, malicious man standing there. I hoped so.

With shaking hands, I removed Watcher's collar and harness. He lapped my face and whined a bit—as if he knew something was wrong. "Go with the man, my sweet boy. I will come back for you soon."

53
"Please, Save My Dog!"

Captain Lichtenberg invited us to stay at his apartment on the outskirts of town, and we accepted, having no idea where we were or how to speak Danish. I hoped it wasn't far, as I would need his help early tomorrow when we went back for Watcher.

Since Peder lived near Captain Lichtenburg, we waited for a bus at a nearby shopping area. We were all tired, but I could only think about Watcher. Was he afraid in that strange place? Was he whining for me, wondering why I left him? He had never been without me since I adopted him. Even more frightening was the thought of that lieutenant, and his threat of putting my dog down.

The bus came, and we were about to get on, when I backed away. "No! I cannot leave Watcher here. That lieutenant will kill him. I won't leave without him."

Peder, who was already on board the bus, hopped off.

The door closed and there we were, standing in a little group, travel weary, smelling of fish, and grubby from the trip.

I burst into tears, sank to the curb, and put my face in my hands and wept. "Watcher is waiting for me. I promised him I'd get him," I wailed. "He's wondering why I didn't come back!"

The three men with me seemed helpless. "What can we do now? The kennel is probably locked up," Peder said.

"We will go back early in the morning," Captain Lichtenburg reminded me.

"No! I'm going now. The morning may be too late. That lieutenant is sure to get there before us. I am going to get Watcher out of there somehow! Go on without me. I don't care."

Captain Lichtenberg sat on the curb next to me and put his arm around my shoulders. "Let's get something to eat, and then we'll figure out what to do. You are tired and hungry and even worse, you had to deal with that bighead of a German."

"I'm not hungry. I'm not tired!" I could hardly see through the tears. "I just want my dog. My sweet . . . wonderful dog. I need . . . Watcher and he needs me." I sobbed.

Barret sat on my other side and took my hand.

"Barret," I pleaded. "We're in a strange place. Watcher is wondering where we are. Please, tell Captain Lichtenberg we must find him."

"Wendy Vendy," Barret whispered in my ear. "Don't cry. We'll go back for him, I promise."

Captain Lichtenberg sighed. "All right, all right, Karin. We will go back and find him after we eat. You can bring Watcher a sausage or something."

I nodded. "Then let's go quickly." I wiped my eyes and my nose on the bottom of my skirt. The Captain stood up and pulled me to my feet.

We all went to a small home-style restaurant. Captain Lichtenberg ordered a bowl of chicken soup and home-made biscuits for me. "Chicken soup is internationally known to make problems go away." Then he ordered two sausages for Watcher. I was able to smile a little. Captain Lichtenberg was fast becoming another good friend.

But after dinner the men once again suggested we all go home and come back for Watcher in the morning.

"No! I have not changed my mind. I won't go anywhere until I have Watcher with me."

They knew by the firm tone of my voice that I meant what I'd said.

"All right," said the captain. "Let's go to the kennel before it gets totally dark."

Daylight lingered late in the Danish summers, and it had melted into a soft dusk.

We all headed back to the customs office to search for the kennel. As we approached the grounds, I pointed to a sign on a nearby building decorated with pictures of cats, dogs, and rabbits and the word DYRLÆGE in big letters.

"This is a veterinarian," Captain Lichtenberg said. "It's near the port, so it might be where the animals are quarantined when they come into the country."

I tried the front door, but it was locked, and there were no lights on inside.

We headed around to the back of the building and immediately a dog began to bark. "It's Watcher!" I whispered excitedly. "I know his bark."

We came upon an area of dirt and grass enclosed by a tall chain fence. Circling inside the enclosure, barking and whining, was my dog. He looked afraid and nervous, but when he saw us, he bounded to me, banging and jumping onto the fence.

"Watcher, look what we brought you." I broke off a piece of sausage and fed it to him through the chain fence. He gulped it down quickly, his tail wagging like a whirligig.

"How do we get him out of here?" Peder said. "We might get caught."

I tossed another piece of sausage over the fence, and Watcher jumped for it, catching it in his mouth.

"I have an idea." I walked along the perimeter, with Watcher following me on his side of the fence. Halfway around I found a spot where the earth was soft.

"Watcher!" I called softly, hoping no one could hear us or see us. "Here, boy." I held out another bit of sausage and let him sniff it through the fence. "Come, Watcher. Fetch! Come get it." I began digging the ground near the fence with my hands.

Watcher looked at me, his head cocked.

"Come!" I called again, still digging the ground at the bottom of the fence.

It took only a moment for my wise dog to figure it out.

He crouched down, pushed his nose close to the fence, and began to dig wildly with both of his front paws. Dirt sprayed in all directions.

Captain Lichtenberg kept a watch around the corners of the building. "If we get caught . . ." He shook his head.

Meanwhile, Peder gave Barret a blow-by-blow description of how close we were to having Watcher on our side of the enclosure.

I continued scooping the dirt on my side, pulling rocks and stones out to clear the way for Watcher. "Good boy!" I said persistently. "Come on, Watcher, you can do it!"

My dog paused occasionally, looking up at me for praise and encouragement. Then down he went again, just as he did back on Lindenstrasse when he dug under the hedges to the yard next door.

Occasionally Watcher tried pushing himself into his tunnel, his tail sticking out behind him and wagging all the time, but then he would back out and dig some more. With each try, he disappeared for a longer time. Then, under my hands that were also digging away the dirt, I could tell he was close. I scraped away the dirt viciously, opening the hole so he could breathe.

"Keep moving, Watcher!" He pushed through the dirt and then wiggled the rest of his body out to freedom. He stood up unsteadily for a moment and shook the dirt from his coat several times. Then he sneezed, shook again, and leaped toward me, covering my face with kisses.

"Let's get out of here," Captain Lichtenberg whispered, "before we are arrested."

Later we hosed Watcher down with water before bringing him into Captain Lichtenberg's house. Barret and I sat on the steps and rubbed Watcher dry with old towels. Watcher wiggled and lapped my face. Suddenly I noticed something.

"Barret, both of Watcher's ears are pointing up. He's a perfect German shepherd!"

"He is proud of his escape success today," Barret agreed as he felt Watcher's ears. "His ears are standing at attention."

54
Good-Byes in Copenhagen

The next afternoon, Captain Lichtenberg took Barret and me—with Watcher trotting along—to Solstice Jewelry, the store that was on my list of contacts. The captain knew Ingrid and Pier, the owners. I wondered if they might be part of the Danish resistance.

The storefront was made up of shining glass windows; behind them, handmade silver jewelry was on display—necklaces, rings, bracelets—many with unusual gemstones.

A bell jingled as we entered, and the couple, who were studying a catalog and busy on the telephone, looked up and smiled. While we waited, I looked around and wandered into a wing dedicated to the Royal Copenhagen porcelain Flora Danica. I had seen only one piece in my life. Adrie once brought a soup tureen to Mom and told us its value. To have hundreds of pieces of the costly dinnerware in one place was like being in a museum. Each dish, trimmed in twenty-four-karat gold, had a different, hand-made flower on it. I could not tear myself away from the display. The store obviously focused on wealthy customers.

Finally the couple came over to us. "I'm looking for my father, Herr Nelson. Is he here?" I asked them in German.

"Ah! We've been so eager to see you!" the woman exclaimed, her face beaming. "I am Ingrid—and this is Pier, my husband."

I was dismayed—this was not the correct answer! However, Pier immediately nudged his wife and answered, "Herr Nelson has gone to back to Sweden."

"I am Karin, and this is Conrad, my brother."

"We have been so worried about you." Ingrid's face became serious. "We knew you were in Hamburg. We never thought we'd see you after the bombings."

"Hamburg was bombed the morning we left," I said.

The couple looked at each other solemnly. "You were fortunate to have left when you did," Ingrid said. "The firestorms were so destructive that the city was sealed off after the first day, and no one could leave after that."

"The big bombers came, night after night, dropping tons of bombs, along with more incendiaries. Hamburg is destroyed," Pier said sadly.

"Hamburg was a sea of flames, and they think fifty thousand were killed." Ingrid's eyes filled up with tears. "Oh, *mein Gott,* how long will this go on?" she asked dejectedly. "The fires and wind took oxygen away from the air—even inside the bomb shelters, people died."

"The asphalt streets were melting, and human beings

caught on fire then disappeared into the tar, dead," Pier added.

"I hope Otto and Ulla are safe," Barret said.

Pier shook his head. "I've heard nothing more from them."

Ingrid tried to be cheerful. "But here you are safe and sound, and soon you will be in Sweden where there is no war." She took me by the shoulders and looked me over. "You are the image of your mother. So beautiful! I see your dear father, David, too. "

"Now that you are here, I will call my friend Erik," Pier said. "He will take you directly to Sweden. It is not far, you know. Once you get to Helsingør, it's just across the way, as you say in English. Only a few miles across the Sound. Come up to our house, up the stairs, now," he directed. "I will call Erik and we will have a fine Danish *frokost*—lunch—and make plans for your trip."

We ate eagerly. There were three types of open sandwiches, along with a crisp salad. For dessert, Ingrid served apple pastries filled with whipped cream. I knew the luncheon must have cost her many ration stamps, and we treasured the love and generosity she and Pier showed us.

I thought about Frieda and hoped she was safe—and that Adrie did not blame her for my running away. "I haven't had such delicious food since I left Berlin."

"I will wrap these sweets for your trip," Ingrid said, noticing how often I helped myself to the food.

Then I gave her the dark ruby. "This is for you and

Pier—from my father, David, and me. He knew you would help us. So he kept this for you, with gratitude."

After dinner we waited in the living room for Erik. I sat on the sofa with Barret, and my dear, lovable Watcher lay at our feet. For the first time in months I was happy. Tomorrow we would be in Sweden! In just another day I would be able to call Mom and Daddy back in the States. The very thought of hearing their voices choked me up. How grateful we all should be for having such a good friend as Opa. Who knows how many lives he saved, despite danger to himself? What a faithful friend he'd been to the sweet father I never knew. He had safeguarded the jewels that turned out to be our assurance to get to freedom.

Mom and Daddy will love and help Barret. They will find a way to get us both back to the United States. I grinned and patted my dog. *Wait until Daddy sees Watcher!* He had always wanted a beautiful shepherd!

The doorbell rang, and Pier went downstairs to answer it. He came back with Erik, a big, tall man who took off his sailor's cap and shook hands with all of us. "I hope you are able to leave tonight," he said. "We have to drive to Helsingør first. That's where my boat is."

"How far away is that?" I asked.

"Not far, about twenty-five miles—or forty-four kilometers from here," Captain Lichtenberg replied.

"Why do we leave from there?" I asked.

"Helsingør is on the Sound. It is the closest city to Sweden, only a few minutes ride by boat. You can actually see Malmö, Sweden, from the port," the captain answered.

"No one mentioned Helsingør until today," I said suspiciously.

"We don't always know exactly where we'll be going—and even when we do, it's not spoken. Escapes are often spur-of-the-moment, different, and always secret."

I was eager to get on our way. "Come on, Bar—" His real name almost slipped out. "Come on, Conrad," I said. "We're going to Sweden!"

Barret got up and almost stumbled over Watcher. My dog hopped to his feet and leaned against Barret, as if to lead him.

Erik frowned and seemed surprised. "Is this boy blind?" he asked Pier softly.

"*Ja,* didn't you know this?" Pier asked.

"Does he have a Swedish birth certificate?"

"No." I moved closer to the two men. "He left Berlin in a hurry and was unable to get his Swedish documents."

"We have a problem then."

"Why?" I asked, becoming more and more concerned.

"The Red Cross knows you arc both coming, but they will not take a German blind boy unless someone in Sweden will sponsor him," Erik explained. "Does he have a sponsor?"

I suddenly felt cold. "I don't think so."

"Nevertheless, you are both minors. Do you have relatives in Sweden?

"That's why they are going to Sweden. To find their Swedish relatives," Captain Lichtenberg lied.

"If I need a sponsor, I can't enter either," I said.

"You will be allowed in Sweden. You have your papers, and you are not blind. They will have a place for you. It's the boy who won't be allowed in."

Barret heard the concern in our voices. "What is wrong?"

"You are German. You have a country over there—Germany or Denmark. The Swedish government is willing to take in refugees, but they won't take handicapped people, unless they have a sponsor—someone who will guarantee their care and safety. Do you have a sponsor in Sweden?" Erik asked Barret directly.

"No," Barret answered. "No one mentioned it before."

"So many disabled refugees are coming and need special care that it has become too great a burden on the Swedish government. Since you are German, not Swedish, you must have a Swedish sponsor."

There was utter silence. Then Barret asked, "What can we do now?"

"The girl here—Karin—I'll take care of her and her dog," Erik said.

"You mean, you can take a dog into the country, but not a blind boy?" Ingrid looked appalled.

"The dog will need to be quarantined for a few days, but yes, that's the law right now. You will be in Sweden legally," Erik said to me. "The Red Cross has already registered you. I believe your parents have been in touch with the authorities there."

"I won't leave without Conrad," I said firmly. "Absolutely not! He came all this way for freedom, and now, when it's only a few miles away, you have to leave him here?"

"I'm sorry." Erik shook his head. "It's useless to even attempt it. They will only turn him away. Are you coming or not, Karin? If you are, we need to get going."

Barret reached out for my hand. "You have come all this way for freedom too, Karin. Do not quit now because of me. You must go on. I'll try to work things out here."

"We'll get you to Sweden." Captain Lichtenberg nodded vigorously. "We'll smuggle you in if we have to."

"Maybe once Karin is in Sweden, she can be a sponsor," Ingrid suggested.

"She would need to be an adult, a legal resident, and working full time with some sort of bank account. It's impossible, I'm afraid," Erik said.

"I will call Opa. He'll know what to do," Pier said decisively.

"Meanwhile, you and Watcher must go on," Barret insisted.

I looked down at Watcher, who sat by my feet. "How will you get along without Watcher?" I asked Barret.

"I will be fine," Barret answered. "Please go with Erik, Karin. Your parents are waiting to hear from you. You're almost home."

I thought of Mom and Daddy. How eager and excited they will be to know I am safe in Sweden. "I need a few minutes alone with Watcher," I said to Erik.

He shrugged and sat on the couch. "Be quick about it."

I took my backpack and called to my dog. "Come, boy.

Let's sit outside for a little while." Watcher immediately followed me to a back door, where there was a porch and a stairway down to the street. "Sit with me, my sweet dog." He obediently sat by my side.

I put my arms around him and buried my face into his coarse coat. "I love you so much, Watcher. I want you with me forever." My dog wiggled and rubbed his cold nose against my cheek as he licked my face. "Watcher, I don't know what will happen to Barret now. He can't come with us. Here the streets are strange, and Barret doesn't know the way, but you know how to lead him, and where to wait for traffic, and where the steps are—and you will love each other. We trained you so well, my sweet dog, and you are so smart and such a good guide dog, you must stay with Barret and help him until we are all together again—the three of us."

Watcher recognized the words *good dog* and slithered his way close to me.

I was about to lose my best friend and my wonderful dog. I swallowed hard. I didn't want to cry. Not now. *Sacrifices must be made in wartime,* I told myself. *I haven't suffered like the thousands who die every day.*

Nevertheless, for the first time in my life I felt agony, as if my heart were breaking.

I removed Watcher's collar, took out the jackknife, pried off four large jewels, and tucked them carefully into a secret pocket in my backpack. There were four more jewels on the collar for Barret. After I replaced the collar, I patted my dog and stood up. "Come, boy."

We went inside. "I'm ready to go, but I'm leaving Watcher with you, Conrad," I said to Barret.

He jumped up. "No, no—you two belong together. He must stay with you." Barret reached for my hand and pulled me toward him. He put his lips to my ear and whispered, "Wendy Vendy. You must not be alone in Sweden. Please take Watcher with you. I know how you love him, and he will be lonely without you. "

"But he will be happy with you." I kissed Barret on the cheeks and then on his lips. I could taste our salty tears. *I must leave quickly,* I thought, *or I will never go.* I bent down to Watcher again. "Take good care of each other." I tried to sound brave, but my voice trembled. "It won't be long until we are together again."

I hugged everyone good-bye and slipped a gemstone into Captain Lichtenberg's palm.

I left quickly—before I could change my mind—before I began to cry—before my broken heart began to bleed.

55
Escape to Neutral Sweden

I had never felt so completely alone, and neither of us spoke while Erik drove me to Helsingør.

When we arrived, Erik said, "Too bad you can't stay awhile here in Helsingør," he said. "The city is also known as Elsinore. There's even a castle there." Erik waited for me to speak, but I didn't answer.

After a moment he said, "Did you ever read Shakespeare's *Hamlet*? This is where the story takes place."

I began to cry. "I don't really care right now, Erik."

"It's all right, little Karin. I know you're sad about leaving your friends."

We finally reached a hidden beach, where a rowboat had been pulled up onto the sand.

"What is this?" I asked. "Are we crossing over to Sweden in a rowboat?"

Erik laughed. "No. There are strong currents through the Sound. The waters between the Baltic Sea and the North Sea merge here." He handed me a lifejacket. "Get in. I'm taking you out to that boat." He pointed to the shadow of a fishing boat on a mooring.

He rowed out, hooked the rowboat to the mooring, and then helped me climb into the larger boat. He started the engine, and the craft moved slowly through the darkening waters. The ship did not have a deep keel, so Erik was able to keep us close to shore, inside markers, and in passages that were not deep enough for larger vessels.

I sat on the deck, covered in a big blanket, and watched the dim shore of Denmark slip away. Darkness had finally settled in, but the sky in the north was alight with aurora—shades of red and green, twisting and dancing. Ahead were the lights of Sweden. Had Barret and Watcher been with me, I would have delighted in the beautiful sight. However, nothing could delight me tonight. Barret and Watcher were on the opposite shore.

Erik turned off the engine and we drifted quietly.

"What's happening?" I whispered.

"Patrol boat—their running lights are dim—over there. See?" He pointed then handed me binoculars.

Sure enough, the shadow of a ship lurked in the darkness. Only the Northern Lights exposed the ship's silhouette.

"They may see us, so be prepared. Sweden is just ahead."

"Will the patrol boat stop us?" I shuddered as I recalled

the German ship and the lieutenant who had accosted us.

We waited, drifting quietly, as the Northern Lights danced in the sky. I opened the parcel of pastries that Ingrid packed and shared them with Erik.

Erik started the engine again and I watched from the bow, as the bright shore of Sweden grew closer.

We were soon tying our little boat to the great docks among the big ships, small ships, sailboats, and fishing vessels. I was in Sweden.

Once we landed, Erik brought me to customs and the office of the Red Cross. "They will take care of you from now on," he said.

I put a jewel in his hand and said good-bye.

"God save you, little girl Karin," he whispered. Then he was gone, and I was alone in a strange country.

A matronly woman at the desk looked up and spoke to me in what I supposed was Swedish.

"I speak only English and German," I told her in both languages. She understood, because she asked my name in English.

"My name is Karin Nelson," I answered.

She looked at a long list and then smiled. "Ah, here it is. Do you have your Swedish identification?"

I opened my rucksack and fumbled through the many things that were in there. "Here is my Swedish birth certificate," I said.

"Ah, good!" Once again I watched as her eyes and fingers drifted down a long list of names. "Karin, your family has arranged for you to stay at a local hostel—a lodging house for refugees." She stood up and pointed to a Red Cross van parked outside the door. "They will take you to your residence," she said, smiling. "But before you go, I have a request from your mother."

I stood silently. Had Adrie found me?

"It's an overseas call, from your parents in the States, so it might take a while. They wanted us to call them as soon as you arrived." She dialed a number on the telephone—spoke a few words—then said, "Go rest on the couch over there until I can connect with your parents."

I sat stiffly on the sofa. All I could think about were Barret and Watcher—only a few miles away in Denmark—but they were another world away from me. Would I ever see them again? Families and friends who were separated and displaced might never see each other, I had been told.

After what seemed like a long while, the woman at the desk called my name and handed the telephone to me. "A call to you from New York," she said, smiling.

"Hello?"

The static was loud and crackling. "Oh, darling! Is it really you, Wendy?" It was my mom's voice—warm and full of love. She was crying.

Then a man spoke: "Honey, it's Daddy."

"Mommy and Daddy." I wept. "I love you both, and I've missed you so much. And now I'm coming home!"

⊙

Epilogue

It was the spring of 1946, and I was curled up in the little gable window seat of my family home in Derry, New York. The war ended last year when both Germany and, later, Japan surrendered unconditionally. As I gazed out the window and watched kids ambling home from school, chasing and teasing one another, I mourned the loss of my own teenage childhood. War took away childhoods and loved ones. War made us grow up too soon.

I would be nineteen in July this year. Barret would have been twenty-one.

Daddy said I should write a book about my escape from Germany to Sweden, then to England, and finally my trip home across the Atlantic—this time safely on the deck watching the sparkling sea and the peaceful nighttime stars. Maybe I would write a book someday—but that would be another story for another time.

Hitler was dead. He supposedly committed suicide just before the Russians invaded Berlin. His great one-thousand-year dream was really a twelve-year nightmare. That cruel, insane Himmler, who had instituted Lebensborn and the death camps, tried to escape by disguising himself as a lowly soldier. When he was found out, he took his own life rather than face the justice that awaited war criminals. Justice came eventually, often in strange ways.

Mom and Daddy worked tirelessly to get me home. Since then we spent hours trying to trace my friends. Thankfully, Daddy had been able to locate most of them, but he was unable to locate Barret.

Every night since we had separated, I heard Barret's teasing whisper, "Wendy Vendy," and my dog's cheerful bark. I pulled the pillow over my head to block out the voices, but they were not silenced.

We were finally able to find Frieda's address in Bavaria. I wrote to her several months ago. Mail is slow and often returned with *Could not be delivered* or *Displaced Person* stamped on the envelopes. However, last week I had an answer from Frieda. The letter was in German.

My dearest little Wendy,

I have prayed for you so many times, and now at last I received your most welcome letter. It was forwarded to me here in Bavaria. I am happy to hear that you are back in your home in America.

For the last two months, I have been living in a friend's home here. She lost her son and husband during the war. We are both glad to be away from the destroyed cities and the sadness. It is beautiful here with the mountains around us. Still, Germany has changed forever. Berlin—and Germany itself—is divided among the Americans, British, French, and Russians, as you probably know.

I am sure you are concerned for Adrie. When she discovered you were gone she was extremely angry. Later she sat down at the kitchen table, put her head in her hands, and sobbed, so concerned for you she was, and the dangers facing you. As time passed, she seemed to accept the fact you were gone—and, hopefully, safe in Switzerland. (That is where she thought you might be. She tried to locate you there.)

You may already know, Adrie was eventually arrested for her part in war crimes. She will be in prison for five to seven years. She is alive and who knows? Perhaps she will eventually grasp what horrors the Nazis brought upon the entire earth. You will hear from her before long, I am sure. She loves you in her own way, you know.

Surprisingly, Admiral Canaris, Adrie's chief and head of Abwehr, was murdered by the Nazis. Come to find out, he was helping the Resistance all along. Life is strange. One never knows how things will turn out.

I hope we will meet again, darling, in a peaceful world.

Love always,
Frieda

Sometimes bad news did not come in the form of a letter. I found out in the newspapers that in 1944 there was an attempt to assassinate Hitler. Several Nazi officers—trusted officials—were indicted and hanged—among them, my borrowed, wonderful grandfather, Opa. I will never believe he had any part in the conspiracy. He hated what was going on in his Fatherland, but he would never kill or hurt anyone. His only crimes were helping Jews and others to get out of Germany. Hitler avenged himself by cruelly hanging anyone even remotely involved with the group of assassins. So my kind, wonderful, borrowed grandfather, Opa, was gone.

I worried about Johanna until Daddy discovered that the Bible Students in Germany—the *Bibelforscher*—were free at last, and held a convention in the very stadium in Nuremburg where Hitler vowed to eliminate them. We contacted the Bible Students in the United States and were told Johanna and the rest of her family were free. Fortunately, Johanna now lived in West Germany. However, many of the Bible Students in Russian East Germany were arrested and sent to Siberia for preaching their religion. I have written to Johanna, and I know I will hear from her.

We were able to find out something about everyone,

except Barret and Watcher. Despite all the hours, and calls, letters, and telegrams we sent, trying to locate them, Barret's whereabouts remained a mystery. Sometimes, I'd hear a dog barking outside, and I would fill up with tears.

"Would you like a German shepherd puppy?" Daddy often asked. "We'll get one anytime you say."

"No dog could ever replace my Watcher," I'd tell him.

Daddy never quit searching for Barret. He contacted every charity, lists of displaced persons in several countries, and even the prisoners who were in concentration camps and who were still living. Daddy and Mom knew very well how much Barret meant to me, what a good friend he was, and how alone he must have been since Opa died.

"Wendy, honey, sometimes we have to accept things that hurt us in order for the pain to finally go away," Mom has said many times.

I was gradually realizing I might never find out what happened to Barret and Watcher.

A couple of weeks ago Daddy went to New York City—which he did sometimes for his work. One morning Mom had an idea. "Dad is coming home tonight. What do you say we plan a special dinner for him?"

Mom made Daddy's favorite—a standing rib roast with baked potatoes. I made the New England clam chowder that Adrie had served at the inn in Maine. I baked a chocolate cake with white butter frosting and wrote *I love you* in chocolate icing on the top.

Everything smelled so good, and I knew Daddy would

be delighted with our surprise. He had tried so hard to make me happy, searching for the few friends I had and lost. He was gloomy when he could not find a clue about Barret, because he hated to disappoint me.

"It's time to let go of the sadness and move on," Mom said.

"I won't beg Daddy to search anymore," I told her. "Perhaps it's better that I don't know what happened to Barret or to Watcher."

That afternoon I was in the kitchen when Daddy's car pulled into the driveway.

Mom peeked into the kitchen—and to my surprise, there were tears in her eyes.

"Is everything all right?" I asked anxiously.

"Dad's home. Go on out and greet him." As she gently pushed me toward the front door, I heard the car doors open, and a dog barking.

"Did Daddy buy a dog?" I asked.

"You know he always wanted a German shepherd," Mom replied as she opened the front door wide. "Your dad always wanted a son, too—and what do you know—I do believe he found one of each!"

A sweet familiar voice called to me, "Wendy Vendy!"

At first I froze. I could not speak or move. Then I flew out the door, my feet never touching the ground. I flew down the flagstone walk to the front gate, and I flew into Barret's arms while Watcher jumped around us, barking joyfully, his tail wagging like a windmill in a gale.

Afterword

If you have read my book *Shadows on the Sea*, you have already met Wendy Taylor when she was vacationing in Maine in 1942. She was a strong secondary character in that story, and at the end, she disappears with her newly discovered mother, Adrie. Readers often write to me asking, "What happened to Wendy?"

In *The Watcher,* we catch up with Wendy in Nazi Germany. Her mother, Adrie, a zealous Nazi, requires Wendy to renounce her former life as an American and become the perfect German daughter.

Historically, Nazi Germany was the epicenter of a true horror story where the unthinkable—known as the *Holocaust*—actually *did* happen. This was when the "Final Solution" was initiated, the plan to exterminate the entire Jewish Race. There were thousands of individuals of various religions and ethnic groups that were also persecuted and there are thousands of true stories yet to be written about them.

As I created *The Watcher,* I wove true historical facts into my plot to show how Nazis also turned their evil obsessions upon *three* other groups.

1) *Lebensborn* (meaning "fountain of life"), was formed by Heinrich Himmler in 1935, where he hoped to create a perfect race of children who would one day rule the world. The children of the Lebensborn program were born of blond, blue-eyed German mothers. Their handsome fathers were *Schutzstaffel* (SS) officers, who were already approved as having German forbears for many past generations. The children born to them belonged to and were under the protection of the SS. Thousands of children were born in the Lebensborn program. Others, who were blond and blue-eyed, were stolen from countries such as Czechoslovakia and Poland—like Hunfrid in my story.

After the war ended, the Lebensborn children who were born in occupied countries were ill-treated because of their German heritage. For example, ten thousand or more children were born to Norwegian mothers and German fathers. However, when World War II ended, many of their offspring were homeless, orphaned, and victimized. It was not until the year 2000 that the prime minister of Norway formally apologized for the cruelty shown to this group.

I was shocked to discover the concept of Lebensborn originated in California decades before Himmler's project. http://hnn.us/article/1796

There were many Lebensborn Homes around Germany and other countries. However, I could not find one in Berlin. So I created a home there to introduce Johanna to the plot, and to keep the story focused in Berlin.

2) I have used the *Bibelforscher* in my story as another group that was mercilessly victimized by Nazis. Bible Students were also known in Germany and around the world as Jehovah's Witnesses.

Wendy's new friend, Johanna, represents this Christian group of German citizens who could not conscientiously take part in the war efforts or the armed services. They considered themselves as citizens of God's coming kingdom and obeyed the Biblical command, "We must obey God as ruler, rather than men." They would not salute *(Heil)* Hitler as their savior. Most stood firm and were either executed or sent to concentration camps and forced to labor, where they were required to wear the purple triangle to identify them. Amazingly, all they had to do was sign a paper renouncing their religion and they could go free! Very few took that way out.

The *Bibelforscher* kept in constant contact with the world outside, bringing news of the concentration camps, murder of Jews, and persecution of Christians via their *Watchtower* magazines, which were smuggled in and out of Germany through hidden mountain paths at midnight or in a myriad of other ways. Although they were few in number, their steadfastness angered the SS and Hitler obsessively. "We will wipe out this brood from the face of the earth," he vowed.

A wing at the Holocaust Museum in Washington, DC, is dedicated to the *Bibelforscher*—Jehovah's Witnesses—for their firm stand against war and the fierce persecution they endured. Documentaries and videos of *Jehovah's Witnesses Stand Firm Against Nazi Assault* can be found at the U.S. Holocaust Memorial Museum site: ushmm.org. Several other documentaries and videos are available on the Internet. Search for "Jehovah's Witnesses Stand Firm Against Nazi Assault." For more information, visit JW.org.

3) A question has hung over Germany and the world since that dreadful war: Why did the German people tolerate the horrors of the death camps, the final solution, euthanasia, etc. in their country? The White Rose resistance group was a group of German students who did speak out against the Nazi regime. These young people felt it was the duty of citizens to stand up against an evil regime that sent hundreds of thousands of its own citizens to death. So they spoke up anonymously. When they were found out, they were given a show trial by the fanatic judge Roland Freisler, who ordered their execution by *Fallbeil* (a German variation of the French guillotine).

Today the German nation recognizes the White Rose group's courage and levelheaded reasoning during a time when logic, choice, and freedom were lost. A statue honors them in Munich and the government has issued stamps to memorialize this brave group of German young people. You can read about them at: jewishvirtuallibrary.org /jsource/Holocaust/rose.html.

Acknowledgment and Appreciation go to . . .

My amazing daughter, friend, and advocate, Deborah Balas, for her TLC and encouragement as I underwent surgery and worked on this story as well.

Kristan, Stephanie, Jennifer, Lisa, Scott, and Judy—for visits, calls, goodies, and the joy that kept my writing muse alive and glowing.

Gabriele Mues, MD TAMHSC Baylor College of Dentistry, and her expertise in the mystery of the missing tooth.

Marita Smith, for translating much of my text into German. *Ich liebe dich!*

The Holocaust Museum in Washington, DC, and the Jewish Virtual Library, who, through their programs and archives, keep the history of the Holocaust alive in the hope that such horrors will never happen again.

Ruta Rimas, my talented and considerate editor. Cheers!

Claire and Larry Krane, who made sure I ate well as I journeyed to 1942 Germany. Thank you, as always, for affection and friendship.

My writing group: Thanks for your candor and support over the years.

Congratulations to June Estep Fiorelli, for her new book, *Stuck Toast and Mud Pies: Poems For Kids*; Gail E. Hedrick, for her award-winning book, *Something Stinks!*; and to Elizabeth A. Conard for her book, *Tori and the Terrific Tiger*. My, aren't we the creative bunch?

My Pi Iota Gamma sorority sisters, for listening patiently to my breathless and continual chatter about World War II history—a group hug is coming up!